A
Harlequin
Romance

OTHER
Harlequin Romances
by FLORA KIDD

Many of these titles are available at your local bookseller,
or through the Harlequin Reader Service.

For a free catalogue listing all available Harlequin Romances,
send your name and address to:

HARLEQUIN READER SERVICE,
M.P.O. Box 707, Niagara Falls, N.Y. 14302
Canadian address: Stratford, Ontario, Canada.

or use order coupon at back of book.

THE CAVE OF THE WHITE ROSE

by

FLORA KIDD

HARLEQUIN BOOKS   TORONTO
WINNIPEG

Original hard cover edition published in 1972
by Mills & Boon Limited, 17 - 19 Foley Street,
London W1A 1DR, England

SBN 373-01663-8

Harlequin edition published February 1973

Printed in Canada

CHAPTER ONE

THE bride and bridegroom were going away. Juliet Grey stood on tiptoe and tried to see over the broadcloth-covered shoulder of the man who stood in front of her and who was effectually blocking the front doorway of the Ring o' Bells, the old coaching inn where the wedding reception was taking place.

It was useless. He was too tall and too wide. He took up all the space. He was deaf too. She'd asked him twice to move and let her pass him so that she could join the laughing, joking group of relatives and friends who were saying goodbye to the happy couple, but he hadn't heard her.

She should be there out in front to wave to Hilary, her lively goodnatured cousin who had married Ian Munro that afternoon in the thirteenth-century church on the other side of the village green. Coming from the Highlands of Scotland, quietly-spoken and a little shy, Ian had come to work for Hilary's father over a year ago. Perhaps it was his native reserve and his obstinate refusal to be stampeded by his boss's gay daughter which had appealed to Hilary, mused Juliet romantically, for she knew that her cousin had fallen head over heels in love with the young, highly-qualified engineer.

Now they were going away together for a honeymoon in Europe and Juliet was determined to wish good luck to the cousin who had remembered her and had invited her to attend the wedding.

'Excuse me, please.' She spoke as loudly as she could. 'I'd like to see them go.'

This time the man in front of her heard. He turned. She was strangely and tinglingly aware of the cold glitter of light eyes, deep-set under dark eyebrows, of a broad chest only just confined by the severe tailoring of an impeccable morn-

5

ing suit, and then she had slid past him, graceful and cool in her sea-green dress.

She was only just in time. Ian had started the engine of the car and Hilary was giving her parents a last kiss and hug before getting into her seat beside her husband. Juliet had to push a little before she was able to get anywhere near the car, and then at last she was standing beside her other two cousins, Hilary's twin sisters Anthea and Sylvia.

Before the car moved away Hilary opened the window on her side and threw her bouquet of red and white roses towards the group of young women. Her sweet, infectious smile lit up her face.

'Here,' she cried, 'whoever catches it will be the next to marry!' Juliet wasn't conscious of striving to catch that bouquet. Like her cousins she held out her arms, but having always been a butterfingers she didn't think she would catch it, so that no one was more surprised than she when her hands closed round the sweet-smelling bunch of flowers with its long trailing ribbons. She gazed down at them in a bemused fashion, only half aware of her cousins' envious comments.

The car was going to the accompaniment of waves and cheers. Aunt Faith, Hilary's mother, superbly elegant as always in navy blue and white, was dabbing at her eyes with a lace-edged handkerchief. Uncle Clive, short and vigorous, his expansive smile a more studied masculine counterpart of his daughter's, was informing the guests that the party wasn't over yet and that there was plenty of champagne left.

And then suddenly everyone had gone, back into the inn, and Juliet was alone in the afternoon sunshine which filtered through the leaves of the sycamore trees edging the green, and she was looking down through a mist of tears at the bouquet of roses.

Still blinded by the tears, she turned and walked reluctantly into the dim interior of the inn. Now that Hilary and Ian had gone her interest in the wedding waned. She would have liked to have escaped from the reception, but she knew that if she didn't join the party, comments would be made about her by Aunt Faith, and she wasn't having that.

It had been a lovely wedding, she thought, Hilary had looked almost regal in a simple dress of white lace. Sunlight had mellowed the grey stonework of the church which was famed for the brasses set into the floor of its aisles. From the carved oak choir stall the voices of the boys had soared heavenwards in perfect harmony, backed by the throbbing sound of one of the finest organs in the country. The reception after the service, held in the elegant, panelled dining-room of the eighteenth-century inn, widely known for its excellent cuisine and cellar, had gone off without a hitch.

In fact it had been everything a wedding should be, as Aunt Faith had intended it should be; a wedding which the county would not forget in a hurry, as Aunt Faith had intended it should not; a wedding which had been as much a testimony of Aunt Faith's severely-conventional outlook and brilliant powers of organisation as it had been the crowning ceremony of Hilary's and Ian's love.

Crash! Juliet's thoughts splintered in all directions. She had walked into something rock-like and resistant. The tinkle of glass warned her that something had broken, and a faint feeling of dampness in the vicinity of her knees made her realise that whatever had broken had contained liquid which had split on her dress; her beautiful dress on which she had spent all her savings.

Shock drove the last glimmer of tears from her eyes and alerted her. Her glance travelled up, over a pale grey waist-coat fastened with pearl buttons, past a pale grey cravat to the edge of a square chin. Above the chin a contradictory mouth was curved into a faintly contemptuous smile. The mouth was contradictory because its long thin upper lip hinted at sternness and possibly cruelty, whereas the full lower lip hinted at generosity and a love of life.

Juliet didn't allow her glance to go any higher than the contradictory mouth.

'I'm sorry,' she muttered to the crushed bouquet in her hand, which looked distinctly forlorn after its contact with that formidable physique. 'I wasn't looking where I was going.'

'You can say that again!'

The voice was a surprise, as was the expression he used. It was quiet and edged by a crispness of accent which she couldn't place.

'Were you blinded by tears, perhaps?' he added, and there was a sarcastic taunt implicit in the words.

But Juliet was impervious to that kind of taunt. Astonished that he had been able to guess so accurately, she looked higher into pale grey eyes bright and observant between thick dark lashes. Above the eyes a lock of dark hair had slid forward on to a lined forehead. It seemed to her to be completely out of keeping with the rest of his immaculate appearance, a symbol of rebelliousness against conventional surroundings.

'Supposing I was?' she replied earnestly. 'People always cry at weddings. They were tears of happiness. Hilary is my cousin and I'm happy because she's happy.'

'And what about the groom? Are you happy for him too?'

'Oh yes, of course I am. Hilary is one of the nicest people I know. Ian can't help but be happy with her.'

'You astound me,' he jibed softly, but didn't say why. 'So you're the cousin of the bride—and incidentally, the only unmarried woman who hasn't been introduced to me yet by my very attentive hostess.' His grey eyes flickered sardonically in the direction of Aunt Faith, who was busy talking to Sir Humphrey Bartlett, chairman of the group of engineering companies of which Uncle Clive was the managing director. 'I wonder why she left you out?' This time the grey eyes subjected her to their all-assessing glance.

'I expect it's because I'm not very important,' Juliet replied in all sincerity. 'I'm only Juliet Grey, the poor relation. If you'll please excuse me I'll go and find someone to sweep up this mess.' She indicated the smashed champagne glass on the floor.

'There's no need. Someone is already coming to do that,'

he said.

His hand was gripping her arm above the elbow and she was unable to move away without pulling in an undignified manner. She looked up enquiringly.

'You don't dress poor,' he remarked. 'That outfit must have set you back a bit.' His bright gaze roved over the sea-green gown with its deep U-shaped neckline, its high waist and long full sleeves, edged with embroidered white roses.

'Yes, it did,' she replied equably. 'All my savings. I wanted to look my best for Hilary.'

'Even though the coffers were empty and the prospects were nil?' His astuteness took her breath away.

'How do you know?' she asked sharply, her eyes wide and wondering.

He touched the fine bones which showed through the white skin where her neck joined her shoulders. The tips of his fingers were slightly rough and their touch embarrassed her and she tried to draw away. But his other hand still held her arm firmly.

'Too thin,' he remarked. 'And I watched you eating earlier.'

'Oh!' The knowledge that those brilliantly-lit observant eyes had been watching her when she hadn't noticed startled her.

'Don't think I don't understand what lies behind your effort to put on a brave show. I once did the same, and turned up at a wedding all correctly dressed, without a penny in my pocket,' he said, and the undercurrent of laughter in his voice mocked himself. 'It's odd what youthful pride will drive us to do. But your beautiful dress is stained. You must let me pay for the cleaning of it.'

'Oh, no, I couldn't! I mean, I don't know you, and it wouldn't be right. It was my fault and I . . .'

'Yes,' he agreed aggravatingly, 'come to think of it, it was your fault. Then come and drink champagne with me and I'll introduce myself, if you insist on being conventional.'

She had the oddest feeling that she was being swept off

her feet by a ruthless force which would push her along remorselessly in the way it wanted her to go, irrespective of any feelings she might have on the matter.

She considered the recalcitrant lock of black hair and then the bright glitter of the grey eyes and came to a conclusion.

'No, thank you,' she said. 'You've quite obviously had more than enough already.'

He was puzzled. 'Enough what?'

'Enough champagne. Now, please let go of my arm.'

By way of answer he let out a shout of laughter which caused every head in the room to turn in their direction.

This time she felt anger scorch through her.

'Oh, now look what you've done! Everyone is looking at us,' she hissed at him.

'Including your aunt, and her expression is one of disapproval, but of you, not me,' he answered, with a wickedly attractive grin. 'So you think I've had more than enough champagne? That's a pity, because I was looking forward to drinking the happiness of the newlyweds with you and at the same time becoming better acquainted with you. You see, I saw your mother dance when I was a boy. It was before you were born. She was dancing the part of Juliet in Lambert's ballet of *Romeo and Juliet*. I guess you were named after her favourite heroine.' He tipped his head to one side and studied her. 'You're not unlike her. Do you dance too?'

'No, I don't. Oh, do tell me about her,' she urged, forgetting that she wanted to escape from him.

'Only if you promise to drink champagne with me.'

She promised, and from then on he took over. Not that he wouldn't have done anyway, she thought ruefully, as she sat on the cushioned window-seat which curved under a bow window at one end of the big room. He was the sort of man she detested, typical of the big business executives with whom Uncle Clive associated; the sort who would always manage to get his own way using any means available to him. But she would sit with him for a while because she wanted to hear about her mother.

When he came with two glasses of champagne he presented hers to her with an amused tilt of his dark eyebrows.

'With the compliments of your uncle. He's very pleased that I'm entertaining his niece, even though his wife frowns upon us and would prefer to see me entertaining one of her daughters.'

Juliet sent a quick anxious glance in the direction of her aunt. It was true, Aunt Faith was watching her, a faint frown of irritation on her usually blandly smiling face, which meant she didn't like what she was seeing.

'Why should Uncle be pleased because you're entertaining me?' Juliet asked, raising innocent eyes to his face. 'Who are you?'

'If you're the poor relation of the Greys, I suppose I might be considered the wealthy relation of the Munros, so watch out, you'd better not offend me,' he remarked with a laugh. 'I'm Lance Crimond.'

Juliet was really none the wiser. The name Crimond meant nothing to her.

'Lance for Launcelot?' she enquired.

'Yes, but spelt with an "a" only. Your turn to laugh and to tell me that you've never met anyone less like a knight in shining armour than I,' he replied, and his wicked white grin was in evidence again.

'Although Lancelot was the warrior whom King Arthur "loved and honoured most" he didn't always behave himself,' murmured Juliet, recalling the stories she'd read of the Arthurian legend. 'He broke a few rules.'

The quick upward glance of his grey eyes was as bright as a flash of lightning against the darkness of a thundercloud.

'And you think I'm capable of doing the same?' he queried with dangerous softness.

'Not only capable, but probably you have already,' she answered coolly. The lightning flash was brighter and she quailed a little at her own temerity. But he didn't retaliate. Instead he laughed again and once again heads were turned

11

curiously, and she wished she hadn't agreed to sit and drink champagne with him.

'We're forgetting our toasts,' he said easily, raising his glass. 'To the happy couple, to Hilary and Ian.'

'To the happy couple,' repeated Juliet, and sipped the sparkling wine.

She glanced at the crushed roses on her lap. *Whoever catches them will be the next to marry.* Would it be her turn next? Would she ever meet anyone who would love and cherish her? Would the loneliness she had known for so long ever come to an end?

'Will you be the next to marry?' said a quiet crisp voice beside her. Now she was convinced he had magical powers.

'You should have been called Merlin, not Lancelot,' she said sharply.

'Nothing magic about it. You looked down at the bouquet and it was easy to guess what you were thinking from the expression on your face. Will you be the next?'

'How do I know? I have no magical powers and can't see into the future.'

'Does that mean you're not in love with anyone?'

'Can't you tell by the expression on my face?' she countered acidly, and his grin appeared again.

'I wondered when you'd show your claws. So you're not in love. For that I'm glad, because it will save complications later on.'

What on earth did he mean by that? She was about to burst into speech when he held up his hand and said quickly,

'I know, I know, don't say it. I'm infuriating, and I've had more than enough champagne. But what else is there to do at a wedding if you're not the bride or the groom except to keep on drinking their health?' He twisted his empty glass in his hand and added sombrely, 'Last time I went to a wedding I vowed I would never go to another.'

'Whose wedding?' asked Juliet, her interest caught by his unusual statement.

'My brother Gareth's,' he replied brusquely.

It was incredible. First Lancelot and now Gareth. Was it possible that Gareth's wife was called Lynette? Juliet longed to ask, but a certain grimness about the set of her companion's mouth suggested that the subject of his brother's wedding was forbidden ground.

'Then why have you broken your vow and come here to-day?' she asked instead.

He considered her slowly and deliberately before he answered.

'To look for a wife,' he replied, and cocked a quizzical eyebrow at her. 'Interested?'

Again anger scorched through her like a flame. She gathered the bouquet in her hand and stood up.

'Now I'm sure you've had more than enough!'

His hand grasped her elbow again and she was forced to sit down on the cushioned seat.

'You'll have everyone looking at us again if you behave like that,' he cautioned derisively, 'and you know how much you dislike drawing attention to yourself. Besides, I haven't told you about your mother yet.'

Out of the corner of her eyes Juliet could see that Aunt Faith was gradually approaching the window seat, stopping every so often to talk graciously to guests.

'Relax,' murmured her companion. 'I'll behave, and I'll deal with your aunt when she comes.'

He noticed too much, she decided, but she leaned back and fiddled with the bouquet. The petals of one rose fell suddenly and lay like crimson drops of blood on the aquamarine sheen of her dress.

'Was my mother a very good dancer?' she asked diffidently.

'To my ten-year-old eyes she was the perfect Juliet, slight and graceful with a cloud of fair hair,' he answered soberly. 'It was my first visit to the ballet—or to any theatre for that matter. My mother is an English Literature buff, as you might gather from the names she gave to her three sons. My youngest brother was christened Tristram. That year she decided to take Gareth and me with her on

13

her annual pilgrimage to the London theatre. The ballet was thrown in for good measure because it was *Romeo and Juliet*, and also because she knew your mother. They both came from the same part of Wales. Did you never see her dance?'

'Not that I can remember. I was only five when she died. How did you know I'm her daughter?'

'Your uncle told me. When I saw you come into church this morning I thought I was seeing things. You resembled her very much, and I was sure you must be related to her. So at the earliest opportunity I asked Clive about you and he told me the whole sad story, how both your parents were killed when they were staying with friends on a sea-going yacht at Monte Carlo. I believe it was a gas explosion, wasn't it? He also told me that he'd brought you up as if you were one of his own daughters.'

'Yes, Uncle Clive has always been very kind. He has a great sense of family,' she replied woodenly.

'More credit to him then. But why did you leave his home to fend for yourself?'

How could she tell him of the unhappy years she had endured living with Aunt Faith? How could she describe Aunt Faith's subtle forms of cruelty to her, which were the outcome of jealousy of the beautiful unconventional Norma who had married the equally unconventional Lawrence Grey, music-lover and critic for a leading newspaper?

'Have you ever felt rebellious?' she asked.

'Not only have I felt rebellious but I've rebelled many times during my life. But you don't look as if you have an ounce of rebellion in you.' He glanced at Aunt Faith and his eyes twinkled wickedly. 'I gather you rebelled against the establishment and ran away. It must have taken a lot of courage.'

'All I had,' she agreed, and experienced a strange warmth because for the second time he had understood and appreciated her feelings.

'Where did you go?'

'To London, to see my mother's old ballet teacher. I'd

always longed to dance ballet, but neither Uncle Clive nor Aunt Faith encouraged me. When I left school I was sent to a secretarial school. It was taken for granted that I would go to work in Uncle's company in gratitude for being given a home and having my education paid for. But when I'd finished my training and I realised what lay before me ... something burst inside. I couldn't stay any longer with them.'

'So what did you do?'

'Madame Follet told me I was too old to train as a dancer. She ran a rather select ballet school, and she took me on as an assistant to her overworked secretary.' She paused a moment, then added in a sad little voice, 'I was there until Madame Follet died quite suddenly three weeks ago.'

'What happened to the school?' His voice was sharp, interested.

'It's been closed. I've been trying to find another similar position, but it isn't easy. I'm not really a secretary type of person, but I enjoyed the work at the school because being involved with ballet made it seem worthwhile.'

She was aware of a flash of navy blue and white. Aunt Faith was on her way towards them.

'Mr Crimond,' she whispered urgently, 'please don't say anything to my aunt or my cousins about me not having a job. I have reasons for not wanting them to know.'

He nodded absently as if he was thinking of something else, and the warmth she had felt faded. He had lost interest in her problem and she was out in the cold again, on her own.

'Where do you live?' The quick question startled her.

'London—Earl's Court. I moved there when the school was closed.'

'Living in a grimy little bed-sitter, no doubt,' he remarked scathingly. 'How would you like to live in a castle ...?'

'Called Camelot,' she couldn't resist saying.

'I'll drive you back to town and tell you about it.'

15

'Oh, no, I couldn't! I wouldn't dream of imposing on you,' she began.

'Now, Julie, you mustn't monopolise Mr Crimond,' Aunt Faith's throaty voice oozed sweetness. 'I'm sure there are many other people here whom he would like to meet. Remember always, Julie, that it's good manners to circulate at a party. That way no one ever gets bored with your brand of conversation. Don't you agree, Mr Crimond?'

While Juliet cringed over the poor wilted bouquet, Lance had risen politely to his feet. He regarded Aunt Faith with cold eyes.

'No, I don't,' he said curtly. 'Juliet and I have had a most interesting conversation. I'd like to continue it and I want very much to drive her back to town, but so far I've been unable to persuade her to come with me. I wonder if you'd be good enough to assure her that I'm sober, in my right mind and come from a highly respectable and respected family?'

The devil! The infuriating devil! What did he think he was doing? Now she was sure to receive a lecture from Aunt Faith on how not to treat an honoured and respected guest. Her sea-blue eyes flashed angrily and her pale hair belled out as she swung round to face him. But on meeting his steady gaze the hot words which trembled on her lips remained unsaid, and to her amazement she heard Aunt Faith saying,

'How could you think such things, Julie? Of course you must go with Mr Crimond. I can certainly vouch for his respectability. But must you leave so soon, Mr Crimond? Clive and I were hoping you would come back to our home for dinner. Julie could come too—after all she is one of the family, and you could take her up to town later.'

'Thank you for the invitation, but I'm afraid I can't stay any longer. I've promised to meet some business acquaintances to-night. It's my only chance to see them, because I'm off to Germany in the morning,' replied Lance coolly.

'So disappointing,' cooed Aunt Faith, 'but I understand. Perhaps next time you're down this way. Just give Clive a ring. We'd be delighted to see you. Now are you quite sure you want to take Julie? She can always go back by train, you know.'

But he was quite sure, and once again Juliet was conscious of being swept along by an irresistible force. This time it swept her through farewells to her uncle and her cousins, out of the inn and into a dashing dark green car which soon was nosing its way through the village out on to a road which wound between leafy hedgerows and past pale stone farmhouses.

'We'll have dinner in town,' said Lance crisply. 'Will that suit you?'

'I wonder you bother to consult me,' she returned tartly, and he chuckled.

'I guess I hustled you a bit, but I knew that the time had come for me to leave and I had a feeling you didn't want to stay much longer. Was I right?'

'Yes,' she admitted with a sigh. 'You like to be right, don't you?'

'I do, and I am right, nine times out of ten. How long did you work for Madame Follet?'

'Four years. That makes me twenty-two. Is that what you wanted to know?'

'You look and behave younger,' he replied bluntly, and for a while there was silence between them.

Juliet watched the elegantly tailored Oxford countryside roll by the window. Tall trees cast long shadows over green fields. Little more than an hour ago Hilary and Ian had come along this same road on their way to Heathrow, yet because of the strange turn of events it seemed hours since they had left. She glanced sideways at her companion and wondered what he had in store for her next. She had to admit he'd handled Aunt Faith very well.

'The last thing Aunt Faith wanted was for you to drive me into London,' she murmured.

'I know. The invitation to dinner was produced very slickly.'

'And I suppose the business acquaintances you have to

see to-night are fictitious.'

'Not at all. They're staying at the same hotel. They're really friends over from British Columbia, three wild miners on the spree in the swinging city. I promised I'd have a last game of poker with them to-night. They return to Canada to-morrow.'

Canada. Now she was beginning to place that elusive intermittent accent.

'Are you a Canadian?' she asked.

'No. I'm British born and I was reared in Scotland like Ian. But I lived in Canada for the best part of nine years. Does it show?'

'A little. Sometimes in your speech, the expressions you use, and you have a slight accent.'

'And sometimes in my manners, perhaps,' he put in dryly. 'Life on a construction site in the wilds can be pretty rough.'

'Why did you come back?'

'My father was ill. I came back to help him in the family business.'

'What sort of business?'

'Do you mean to say you don't know, that you've never heard of Crimond Civil Engineering or my grandfather Alexander Crimond who designed the Kawali Dam and the Fraser Bridge?' His voice shook with incredulous laughter.

'No, never. Should I have done?' asked Juliet innocently. Now she understood his association with Uncle Clive, whose company supplied equipment to construction companies.

'Oh, this is priceless,' he was still chuckling. 'Tess is going to love you.'

'Tess?'

'My mother. She's a sort of elderly hippy. She's always scorned big business and money-grubbing. She lives in a perpetual day-dream and prefers the simple life as long as someone is willing to foot the bill. She writes—romantic thrillers, I think they're called. Perhaps you've heard of her even if you haven't heard of my illustrious grandfather. Her

18

pen name is Tessa Dean.'

Juliet, who had recently read the latest offering by Tessa Dean, was enthralled by this piece of news.

'I loved her last story. It was fascinating. It was called *Sounding Brass*. But why is she going to love me? I'm not going to meet her.'

'Yes, you are. You're going to have dinner with her, and with a bit of good luck you're going to be her secretary-companion and live in a place which isn't called Camelot.'

Juliet took a deep breath. Somehow she must make an effort to battle against this inexorable force which had entered her life and had taken her over, before it swept her in a direction she didn't wish to go.

'Mr Crimond——' she began firmly.

'If you're going to object you may as well save your breath,' he said curtly, 'because I'm not going to listen. There's the motorway ahead. I like driving fast, but I find it safer if I'm not involved in an argument at the same time.'

After several miles of tight-lipped, fist-clenched silence, Juliet's temper began to simmer down. She wasn't normally a quick-tempered person, but Lance's calm assumption that she should do as he dictated had roused the independent spirit which slept beneath her docile appearance, and it took her some time to control the urge to attack him verbally. By the time she had decided there was little use in speaking to him if he wasn't going to listen and if he wasn't going to retaliate, which for some reason was even more irritating, they were speeding along the motorway towards London, and she was saving her breath.

Save your breath to cool your porridge. The old saying flashed through her mind. Did they eat porridge in the place which wasn't called Camelot? Since it was in Scotland it was quite possible that they did. He had said he would tell her all about the castle while he drove her into town. In fact that had been the bait which had enticed her to come with him, she thought crossly, conveniently forgetting that she had had no choice in the matter but had been hustled into coming with him. And now he was sitting there silent and relaxed, not telling her anything, while the car hurtled along at seventy miles an hour.

Perhaps she would learn more about the castle from his mother who was Tessa Dean, the novelist, with whom she was going to have dinner. Alarm struck. How could she have dinner in a London hotel in this dress on which champagne had been spilt? She leaned forward to see if the stain was bad. It was quite faint and might not be noticed by others, but she knew it was there and she would be conscious of it all the time and it would worry her.

Juliet's eyes gleamed mischievously. Here was her excuse not to go to dinner with Lance Crimond's mother—a way of thwarting this man who thought he had taken over. When they were nearer London she would ask him to take her to Earl's Court so that she could change. Once she was in her own place she would refuse to go on with him, and short of abducting her with physical violence there would be little he could do.

As the sprawling suburbs closed in around them she brought up the subject of the dress.

'I can't go to dinner in this dress,' she announced clearly. 'Why not?'

'It's stained, and it isn't very suitable.'

He flicked a sidelong glance in her direction.

'As an excuse to get out of dining with my mother that's very poor,' he jibed. 'You must know how elegant and mysterious you look in it.'

Elegant and mysterious? That wasn't how she saw herself. She was so interested and puzzled by the different image of herself, wondering how she could possibly have achieved it quite by accident, that several more miles passed before she saw his comment for what it was, a way of diverting her from her intention.

'I must change it,' she insisted. 'It won't take long. I live quite near the Exhibition Hall and I can direct you from here.'

'Nothing doing, Juliet. You're fine as you are. My

mother isn't a stickler for etiquette like your Aunt Faith, and she probably won't care what you're wearing. Ten to one she'll be in tweeds and beads herself.'

After that she gave up and sat in passive silence trying to pretend to herself that she wasn't excited at the thought of meeting Tessa Dean, and that the possibility of becoming her secretary wasn't enticing. If only the opportunity hadn't come her way through this domineering, infuriating man!

Mrs Crimond wasn't staying in the same hotel as her son. She preferred the slower, more conservative ways of an old-established hotel in Bloomsbury to the streamlined, efficient American-style amenities offered further west which were his choice.

At the reception desk they were told that she had already gone in to dinner and had left a message for Lance saying that he was to join her in the dining-room. Attacked suddenly by shyness, Juliet excused herself to go to the ladies' room to freshen up before going to the dining-room.

'You can go if you promise not to try and escape by the window,' said Lance sternly.

'Having come this far I'm not going to be done out of a meal,' she retorted a little shakily, lifting her chin.

'That's better,' he said, and glanced down at the dilapidated bouquet which she was still carrying. He took it from her and examined it. Only one rose seemed to have escaped being squashed. It was a white half-opened bud. Lance pulled it out, stared at it for a second and then to Juliet's surprise tucked it behind her ear.

'I think you might call it symbolic,' he remarked. 'See you here in a few minutes.'

Slightly bemused by his action, Juliet stared at herself in the mirror in the ladies' room. There was a flush on her usually pale cheeks and her eyes were sparkling. The white rosebud looked untouched and curiously innocent against the swathe of her pale hair. Symbolic, Lance had called it. What had he meant? She knew the white rose was one of the Scottish symbols along with the lion rampant and the thistle. Had he meant she should wear it because with a bit

21

of good luck she might go to Scotland as his mother's secretary? Or had he meant something deeper? Who could guess what went on in the mind of a man like Lance Crimond? He was too complex a personality for her to understand. Nor did she wish to understand him.

But even as her hand was raised to remove the rose from behind her ear and to throw it into the waste basket she experienced a sudden bewildering change of mind, and left it where it was.

They found Mrs Crimond sitting alone at a table for two, peering through a pair of owl-like spectacles at the menu. She was a slim straight-backed woman with a mass of wavy white hair. As Lance had said, her attitude to dress was careless and she was wearing a nondescript skirt and blouse which Aunt Faith might have considered suitable for supervising the cleaning of the house. Around her neck were row upon row of multi-coloured beads of which any hippy would have been envious.

When they reached the table and Lance spoke to her she looked up and removed the glasses, and at once the initial impression of someone who was careless and slovenly was dispersed by the high forehead, clear-cut aquiline nose, fine sweep of cheek from temple to chin and the intelligent vivid blue eyes.

'Lance, how lovely! Are you going to dine with me after all?' Her voice was gentle with just the slightest suspicion of a lilting Welsh accent.

'No, but I've brought someone who is.'

Juliet in her shyness had lingered behind him, hiding behind his broad shoulders, but as he spoke he reached out a hand, took one of hers and pulled her forward. Mrs Crimond's blue eyes focused on her and surprise widened them before she transferred her gaze to Lance.

'The young Juliet,' she murmured. 'Where did you find her?'

'At the wedding. And her name really is Juliet—Juliet Grey. She's Norma Thomas's daughter.'

'Oh, my dear!' To Juliet's amazement Mrs Crimond

stood up, grasped her by the shoulders and kissed her on both cheeks. 'This is wonderful! I knew your mother well. Her death was one of the great tragedies. She still had so much pleasure to offer the world. Please sit down—here, near me. Lance, ask them to set two more places. This is a very important occasion and should be celebrated accordingly.'

'Then you shall celebrate it with Juliet. I need to change out of this lot,' replied Lance, indicating his morning suit. 'I promised Eddie and Cal that I'd see them, as it's their last night in London.'

A faint frown expressing supercilious distaste marred Mrs Crimond's high white forehead.

'So you prefer a night out on the town with some of your more uncouth acquaintances to dinner with Juliet and me,' she said with a touch of asperity, and Juliet glanced uneasily at Lance, expecting him to take offence. But he merely grinned affectionately at his mother.

'They're a wild bunch when they're let out on the spree, I admit, but I wouldn't call them uncouth. Rugged, hardworking and entitled to a gay time occasionally, but not illmannered,' he murmured in defence of his friends.

Mrs Crimond's frown faded and her eyes twinkled with understanding.

'All right, I'll let you off this time, but only because you found Juliet and had the sense to bring her to me,' she said, smiling warmly at Juliet, who was immediately enslaved.

'I thought you might see it like that,' said Lance. 'But now that I've found her for you, can I trust you not to let her escape? She has quite a strong streak of independence. It just happens that she's out of work, and I think she's what you've been looking for.'

Mrs Crimond gave him a slightly puzzled glance.

'She types ... and can do secretarial work,' prompted Lance softly, and understanding dawned slowly in Mrs Crimond's eyes.

'Is that true?' she asked Juliet.

'Yes. I've been working as an assistant secretary to

Madame Follet for the last four years.'

'I can hardly believe it! You look more like a ballet dancer to me,' whispered Mrs Crimond. 'You know, Lance, she's like an answer to an oft-repeated prayer.'

'She's been conjured up by old wizard Merlin especially for you, Tess,' he remarked mockingly. He touched Juliet briefly on the shoulder and to her consternation she shivered at his touch. 'I'll say goodbye to you for now. See you in Camelot,' he murmured, and there was a strangely cynical twist to his mouth as if he had noticed her shiver. He turned to his mother and added. ''Bye, Tess, and remember what I said. Don't let her escape.'

'Camelot?' repeated Mrs Crimond as she watched her son leave the room, a shadow of anxiety deepening the blue of her eyes. 'Why does he say he'll see you there?'

'He told me that you'd named all your sons after the Knights of the Round Table, so when he said you lived in a castle I asked if it was in Camelot. I'm afraid I was making fun because of his name,' Juliet explained honestly.

The shadow was routed by the sudden warm smile.

'You're not the first to do that, dear,' said Mrs Crimond. 'Although I don't think your own mother was any less romantic than I when she named you Juliet. You see I was brought up on the Arthurian legend. My father was a professor of Ancient History and he used to spend most of his spare time searching for evidence of the city of Camelot. I used to dream that when I married and had sons I would call them after King Arthur's knights, hoping that they would grow up to be chivalrous and brave. And in spite of the fact that I married a hard-headed, practical Scot who had his own ideas on how his boys should be named, I kept that resolve. Robert finally indulged me in my whim, provided each of the boys was given a good honest Scots name as his first name.'

'And have they grown up to be chivalrous and brave?' asked Juliet, who was enthralled by this story. Its silly romanticism was right up her street.

'I'm going to let you be the judge of that, dear. You've

24

already met Lance.'

'I think he's very arrogant,' Juliet couldn't help saying. 'I had no intentions of coming here, but he made me.'

Mrs Crimond chuckled.

'Yes, he's very like his father in that respect. That's why fur and feathers used to fly whenever they were together, especially after Lance went into the business after he'd qualified as a civil engineer. He thought he knew all the answers and quite naturally Robert took exception at being told how to manage by a young man just out of University. It was fortunate for all concerned that Robert's Canadian associates received a new contract to build a hydro-electric dam at that point and were willing to take Lance to work on the project as a junior engineer. He stayed with it for a while and then went on to work on other projects over there. I think he wouldn't have come back if I hadn't asked him to come three years ago.'

Mrs Crimond sighed suddenly and her eyes went blank as she looked into the past. Juliet busied herself with the menu. A waitress approached and Mrs Crimond came back into the present again and they ordered their meal.

Often afterwards Juliet was to remember the hours spent in the old-fashioned dining-room of the hotel. Mrs Crimond was a skilful questioner and a sympathetic listener, so it wasn't long before she had heard all about Juliet's uncomfortable childhood with Aunt Faith, her slight rebellion and the pleasant years spent in the ballet school.

'What a waste!' sighed Mrs Crimond. 'You should have been a dancer. You are almost the exact replica of your mother, small but graceful, delicate yet resilient, with an air of untouched innocence which was so invaluable to her in the part of Juliet. But instead you're a typist, and above all things I need a typist, but not any typist. I need someone with sensitivity who won't mind living in an old fortified house built on a promontory in a Scottish sea loch; someone who likes young girls such as my granddaughter Maree; someone who won't be disturbed by the sight of a cripple, my son and Maree's father, Gareth.'

'A cripple?' exclaimed Juliet.

'Yes. Didn't Lance tell you about Gareth? I can see he didn't. He thought he'd done enough by bullying you into coming to see me. Gareth was hurt while on a skiing holiday with his wife Moira, almost three years ago. He survived, but only just, and he's paralysed in one leg. Sometimes it's worse than others. Lance says . . .' She caught her lower lip between her teeth as if to stop herself from saying more. 'But then Lance is often unkind,' she added in an undertone. She looked directly at Juliet again. 'Do you think you would like to come and work for me?'

Juliet felt she was drowning. Tessa Crimond's way of stating her case was as effective in its way as her son's high-handedness had been. It was going to be difficult to refuse this offer of a job. The castle, the girl, the cripple, all made their appeal to her romantic outlook on life. She wanted to take the job because she wanted to see them, to find out what they were like.

'Yes, I think so,' she said, hiding her intense excitement under a matter-of-fact façade. 'Where is the castle?'

'Please don't think it's like an English castle, like Warwick or Ludlow. It's really only a house. It's called Castle Ross—Ross is the Gaelic word for promontory. We found it, Robert and I, thirty years ago when on holiday on the west coast. It was roofless and empty, and for sale. Robert bought it and the surrounding land, mostly bare moorland and mountain, and he proceeded with his usual interest in anything to do with buildings to restore it and alter it. Its restoration became his hobby and was a great source of escape from the demands of business life. I only wish he had lived long enough to enjoy his retirement living there.'

There was a little silence as Mrs Crimond thought of what might have been and Juliet finished her dessert.

'I live there all the time now, but I've not been able to persuade anyone to come there as my secretary. Sometimes I think it's because the place is too remote, too far from the bright lights, and sometimes I think it's because Maree lives there with me.'

'How old is she?'

'Just twelve. Gareth was only twenty-one when he married Moira. He and Maree have lived with me ever since Moira was killed last winter in an avalanche in the French Alps. I have to admit that I'm not the best of mothers, I get too absorbed in my writing, but I find Maree a handful—lovable, you know, but definitely a rebel. Of course, the best thing would be for Gareth to marry again and provide her with another mother, but as he says, what woman nowadays is going to saddle herself with a cripple and a child?'

The frown of anxiety had appeared again as a new thought occurred to Mrs Crimond and Juliet waited patiently to hear more.

'Last time he was at the castle Lance, who as I've said can be very unkind to Gareth, suggested that while he was down here in London he should find a wife for Gareth in the same way that he found the last one.'

Startled, Juliet sat up straight, recalling Lance's derisive remark that he had gone to Hilary's wedding to look for a wife and asking her if she was interested.

'Did he really find the last one?' she asked curiously.

'I suppose he did in a way. He met Moira first when he was on a sailing cruise somewhere off the west coast. He brought her home just as he used to bring all his friends home. It was a case of love at first sight with Gareth. But sometimes I've wondered.... But there I go rambling on, when I should be making sure you won't escape. Are you going to come to Castle Ross and help me? I'd like you to come partly because you are your mother's child but mostly because I think you will enjoy living there. I think you'd fit in to our way of life. You wouldn't find it strange as so many would. Having worked for Nina Follet all that time you won't be bothered by displays of temperament, and your experience in dealing with young ballet dancers should be a help in coping with Maree. Now don't commit yourself

27

immediately. You're to think about it while we have our coffee.'

There was really no need for her to think about Mrs Crimond's invitation to go and work for her, thought Juliet, because she was caught, trapped in a spell cast by a wizard called Lancelot Crimond. When she had come to the hotel she had been determined to resist any persuasion on his mother's part. Her determination had its origin in a desire to prove to that arrogant man that he had been wrong in his judgement of her own personality and of his mother's requirements.

But he had been right, uncannily right. The situation at Castle Ross, as outlined by Mrs Crimond, appealed to her. There was only one snag, as far as she could see, and that was the overbearing, enigmatic Lance, whose wisdom frightened her.

It was as if her thought communicated itself to Mrs Crimond.

'I hope you won't let Lance's high-handed behaviour this afternoon influence you too much against us. He's principally a man of action and is the most practical of my sons, and so often he appears ruthless and inconsiderate of other's feelings. But I think his intentions were good on this case. He would be thinking of me and wanting to help you so his main object this afternoon would be for you and me to meet. Once we met he was wise enough to leave us alone.'

'Is Gareth like him?' Two like Lance would be too much.

'Not at all. He's eighteen months younger than Lance and has always been the gentler, more sensitive of the two. Until the accident took away his ability to move about easily he was a lecturer in Political Philosophy and was beginning to be recognised as quite brilliant.'

The faint distressed frown appeared again. 'He could have continued with his work, I'm sure, but the accident plus Moira's death had a very bad effect on him. He stays at the castle all the time and doesn't go out, as if he's afraid to venture into the world in case he gets hurt. But he's begun to write, to my great pleasure. History, of course, and it's just possible you might find yourself typing for him too . . . that is if you decide to come.'

Juliet capitulated at once.

'I shall come. I can't help myself, and your high-handed man of action knew it.'

'Yes,' murmured Mrs Crimond, gazing past her with blank eyes. 'Lance is so often right . . .'

After arrangements had been made for Juliet to travel north two weeks later she returned by taxi to the dingy, badly lit, shabby room in which she had lived since the Follet Ballet School had been closed. It was like returning to earth after a glimpse of heaven, and she was beset by a sudden irrational fear that perhaps she had imagined everything which had taken place since she had walked blindly into a complete stranger at Hilary's wedding reception.

Then she caught sight of herself in the mirror above the sink as she filled a glass with cold water. The white rosebud on its long stem was still tucked behind her ear. Slowly she pulled it out and placed it in the glass. It was a little droopy, but it still retained that look of purity and innocence.

An air of untouched innocence—Mrs Crimond had said that. Juliet examined her reflection. A pale elfin face framed by pale blonde hair and lit by wide and wondering sea-blue eyes which tilted upwards slightly at the corners. Yes, she did look rather innocent. Was that how she appeared to Lance Crimond too? Was that why he had said the white rosebud was symbolic?

As she stared at the mirror her reflected face seemed to dissolve and its place was taken by another. Hawklike masculine features, a lock of dark hair sliding forward on a wide forehead, eyes which glittered with a cold brilliance, a contradictory mouth curved in a faint enigmatic smile. Juliet blinked rapidly and the image faded.

Hastily she turned away from the mirror and began to prepare for bed, telling herself that in spite of reports she

29

had read in newspapers and magazines about modern witches and wizards, witchcraft belonged to the past, to myths and legends such as that written about King Arthur and his knights. She had only seen Lance Crimond's face in the mirror because he had been the most disturbing factor in a very eventful day. He had been disturbing because he had taken control of her life so easily, whisking her away from the elegant ritual of an English wedding to an old hotel, and an interview with his vague, romantic mother.

She pulled back the covers on the bed-settee, shook her pillow and lay down. She switched off the light and lay with her arms under her head watching the reflection from the street lamp outside on the ceiling.

A very eventful day. Looking back over it it seemed to her that when she had waved goodbye to Hilary she had also waved goodbye to a part of her life. Ahead was the future, shrouded in Scottish mist which swirled about the turrets of a fantastic castle inhabited by people with beautiful names—Tessa, Maree, Gareth, who was afraid to go out into the world any more because his leg was paralysed; Tristram who preferred to be known by his Scottish Christian name of Jamie; and Lancelot, who could be unkind to his crippled brother and who preferred actions to words.

He was much more a Jamie than a Tristram, thought Juliet, as the youngest of Mrs Crimond's three sons greeted her in the arrival lounge at Glasgow airport. About twenty-six years of age, slightly shorter than his eldest brother but possessing the same width of shoulder, he was a freckled-faced, friendly young man with placid blue-grey eyes and brown crinkly hair, and he performed the chivalrous task of carrying her luggage out to his car cheerfully and effortlessly.

'I hope you're prepared for a long drive,' he remarked as they settled into the front seats of the car. 'The road from here to Castle Ross is tortuous to say the least. It's actually quicker to go by boat down the Clyde and up Loch Fyne and then overland from Tarbert, but since I'm going there for a few weeks' holiday Mother thought it would be better if I met you and took you there. She had some funny idea that you might get lost on the way. So by road we shall go following the coasts of the great sea lochs as they delve into the mountains. It's a good day for travel ... cool and clear.'

They crossed the River Clyde at Erskine and followed the inland thrust of that long narrow arm of the sea, Loch Long. From Arrochar they turned left and drove westwards along Glen Croe, under the formidable shoulders of a mountain called the Cobbler, so often shrouded in mist but putting in an appearance, as Jamie remarked cheerfully, especially on Juliet's behalf.

Although the road, as he had said, was tortuous, he seemed to know it well enough to keep up a flow of words, not only informing her about the scenery and place names but also managing to slip in a few facts about himself and the Crimond family.

It turned out that he was a geologist, or at least he was taking a post-graduate course in geology at Edinburgh University, lecturing and doing research at the same time. His hobby was speleology, which was the study of underground caves, more familiarly known as potholes.

'Did you know that the world under our feet is almost the only part left unexplored, and that in Scotland, in the north-western part of the country, there was still an extensive cave system unopened?' Jamie didn't wait for a reply to his question but continued to tell her about what was for him a most important activity.

'I've just come from a meeting of the Caving Society in Glasgow. Incidentally, it was founded by my brother Lance and his friend Graham Lee some years ago. Graham is the president and a keen caver. Lance dropped out of the Society when he went to Canada, although he's shown an interest since he returned, and last year he and I had a look at the one limestone thrust we have on the estate at Castle Ross, but it was rather disappointing. After a few weeks at the castle I'm joining Graham's new expedition to the valley of caves up in the north. This year we're hoping to

31

get into the main system . . .'

He chattered on. Juliet found his impersonal manner relaxing and found she was enjoying the drive along the road through Glen Kinglas, round the top of another wide loch to the town of Inverary where they stopped for lunch.

She left Inverary with an impression of one wide street, of sunlit white paint everywhere and pleasant homely hospitality in the George, the old inn where they ate their meal. Travelling southwards for a while they meandered beside the mighty Loch Fyne, placid and dimpling under the summer sun, with the hills of Cowal beyond alternately smiling and scowling as clouds chased each other above them.

After several miles they turned west again along a secondary road which wound amongst moorland scattered with sheep and outcrops of rock. As they twisted and turned Juliet expected to see another loch round every bend or after they had topped another hill, but it wasn't until almost four o'clock in the afternoon that she had her first sight of Castle Ross, romantically mysterious in the glow of afternoon sunshine, its square tower silhouetted on a promontory of rock, dark against the shimmering sheen of Loch Moy.

Then the car dipped down yet another hill between stone walls and the castle was lost to view as the road made a right-hand bend into the village of Lochmoyhead, a single street of whitewashed cottages, glinting in the sunlight against the blue-green of the forest behind them.

Once through the village, the grey and dusty road wound its way some distance away from the rocky cliffs which bounded the eastern side of the loch. On the left-hand side of the road the land rose gently to the craggy ramparts of mountains, and it was planted with small mixed trees.

'Lance's pride and joy,' said Jamie, waving a hand in the direction of the trees. 'He's got a thing about reafforestation, about paying back to the land what has been taken from it by man. Atonement, he calls it. He's spent a lot of money planting acres of trees on the estate.'

32

'I thought the castle and estate belonged to your mother,' said Juliet.

'No. Father left everything, on condition that my mother should be allowed to reside here for the rest of her life, to that unknown quantity, my eldest brother.'

'Why do you call him that?'

'Because he is virtually unknown to me. I was fourteen when he went off to Canada, and all I knew of him before that were the vibrations which went through our home in Glasgow every time he came home from school or university and tangled with my father.'

'But surely he used to come home occasionally from Canada, for Christmas and New Year, and you saw him then,' suggested Juliet.

'Oh, he came home sometimes, but not for the festivities to which you refer. He came at other times and his visits were brief. I never saw him.' He glanced at her curiously. 'I'm told he found you. What does it feel like to be selected from the masses by one of the wealthiest men in this part of the world?' he asked.

'I'd no idea he was as wealthy as all that.'

'No?' There was a touch of unexpected sarcasm in his voice. 'Are you sure? Isn't his wealth the attraction? Isn't that why you've taken the rather nebulous position of secretary-companion to my mother?'

'No, it isn't,' denied Juliet hotly, appalled by his accusation that she was chasing Lance Crimond because he was a wealthy bachelor. 'I've taken the position because I like your mother and because I need a job. It has nothing to do with your brother's attractions, financial or otherwise. I don't like him.'

Jamie's chuckle was an infectious sound.

'Well, you're frank enough. I'm sorry if I hurt your feelings, but you see since my father died and left most of his wealth to Lance, my brother has been subjected to that sort of pursuit from various young women. Not that he hasn't been able to take care of himself. He has. In fact you may have noticed that he has certain inhuman qualities.'

'Inhuman? What do you mean?' demanded Juliet.

She noticed they had turned off the road into a narrower one which curved between spruces, tall and straight, forming a narrow tunnel into which the sun did not penetrate.

'Perhaps I used the wrong word,' explained Jamie, who didn't seem to be at all disturbed by the gloom or by the strange image of his brother which he had evoked. 'Extrahuman would be better, as if he possesses powers beyond those supplied to ordinary mortals.'

Juliet's blood seem to freeze as she recalled the vision of Lance Crimond's face in her mirror.

'You mean ... like Merlin, the magician in the stories about King Arthur?' she whispered.

Jamie's crack of laughter was like the sunlight into which they now drove, warm and cheerful dispersing the chilly gloom.

'You're as bad as Mother! Full of romantic, fantastic fantasies. I suppose that's the Welsh blood showing. No, Lance isn't a wizard in the strict sense of the word and he'd be very scornful if you attributed his abilities to witchcraft. But he's right so often about people and events that it's damned comfortable having him around at times.'

'I think I understand,' said Juliet, feeling a little easier. 'Does he often come to Castle Ross?'

'I suppose you're hoping you're going to escape his eagle eye,' said Jamie, sending her an amused yet sympathetic glance. 'Then I'm afraid you're in for a disappointment. He comes as often as his business commitments allow him and he arrives when he's least expected and puts everyone into a tizzy. He likes to keep an eye on the estate and also on Mother and Gareth. Not that I blame him for watching them. They're both so vague and scatterbrained when it comes to money and business matters that it's no wonder Dad left the administration of their inheritance in Lance's hands. He doles out their allowances. Well, here we are, Juliet, at the enchanted castle where, as in the case of Camelot, you'll find that nothing is as it seems.'

At close quarters, in the warm hazy light of afternoon

sunshine, the castle lost much of its mysterious romanticism. It consisted of a strong stone tower, three storeys high, to which had been added an L-shaped wing. That afternoon, basking in warmth, surrounded by a garden of green shrubs, rose-beds and deciduous trees, with a creeper winding its way up its grey stonework, it looked pretty and idyllic rather than majestic and aloof.

Jamie took Juliet in through the main door, a rather grand affair set in the wall of the L-shaped wing. It was built in the Jacobean style, he told her carelessly, with curved corners to its square arch and a family crest, carved in stone, set above it.

'Not ours,' he added with a cheeky grin, pointing to the crest. 'It belonged to the previous owner who lost his life at the battle of Culloden. We come from more plebeian stock.'

The hallway was wide and had panelled walls and a high ceiling decorated with ornate plaster work. Jamie put down her luggage and let out a yell.

'Anyone at home? Mother ... Gareth ... Vinnie? We're here!'

No one came immediately in answer to his call, so he took her into a room on the left. It faced westward and the only word Juliet could find to describe it was gracious. Long velvet curtains moved slightly at the open French window through which she could see a small stone terrace.

'Sit down and make yourself comfortable while I go and find Mother,' said Jamie. 'I expect you'd like a cup of tea. I could do with one myself. The last part of the drive is exceptionally tedious.'

When he had gone Juliet looked round the room and once again was struck by the mixture of comfort and elegance. It was a room in which to take afternoon tea and yet it was also a room in which to read or sew. There were several watercolours on the walls, mostly depicting scenes of mountains and lochs, and over the fireplace there was an oil-painting of a man dressed in clothes of the Edwardian era, who possessed a pair of remarkably piercing grey eyes. Going over to the picture, she read on the gilt plaque

35

beneath the picture ... his name, Alexander Crimond. Glancing up at the painted face again, she decided that there was no doubt at all as to his relationship to Lance Crimond.

Tempted by the open window, she went across to it and stepped through on to the terrace, and had her breath taken away by the view. Below was the loch, that long water, island-scattered, opening on the distant glittering deeps of the sea. Ahead was a dark bank of hills above which the misty disc of the sun shone.

She stood quietly absorbing the tranquillity of the scene spread before her.

'Admiring our view?' enquired a pleasant voice behind her. 'You'll find none better anywhere in the world.'

Startled, she swung round. A man stood in the window frame, and as soon as she saw him the word's from Tennyson's *Idylls of the King* came into her mind.

> '*The last tall son of Lot and Bellicent,*
> *And tallest, Gareth ...'*

He must be Gareth, not the last son of Tess and Robert Crimond, but the last one for her to meet, and certainly the tallest and most handsome. Brown hair, darker than Jamie's but not as dark as Lance's, waved back from a lean, fine-boned face to which suffering had added its own distinction.

He moved and the impression of lithe grace was destroyed immediately as the stick he used became evident and he dragged his right leg stiffly.

'You must be Juliet,' he said softly, and held out a hand to her. Speechless, Juliet nodded and put her hand in his and felt the warmth of his grasp.

'I'm Gareth Crimond,' he added. 'I believe my brother Lance found you, and as usual I'm astonished by his good taste. Welcome to Castle Ross. I've been looking forward to your coming here.'

36

Bewitched by his voice as much as by his words, Juliet looked up into eyes which were as deeply blue as parts of the loch, and drowned willingly.

CHAPTER TWO

JULIET awoke early, disturbed by the sound of a bird's cry, a long-drawn-out wistful wail. She blinked sleepily at the square of window. It framed a patch of blue sky across which a wisp of white cloud trailed. Slowly she looked round the room, her glance lingering on the pretty antique furniture. Although she had been at Castle Ross almost three weeks she hadn't yet become used to the pleasure of waking in this small room tucked away under the roof of the square tower, and comparing it with the room she had left in London.

Lying there, comfortably drowsy, safe in the knowledge that she wasn't expected to rise for at least another hour, she let her mind drift back over the time which had passed since she had first set foot in the castle and had met Gareth Crimond. The days which had followed that meeting had psssessed a curious dreamlike quality as she had gradually adjusted to the slow pace of life at the castle. No demands had been made on her, because Mrs Crimond didn't require her to type just yet as she was still immersed in the composition of the first chapter of her new book, and because Maree, Gareth's daughter, was away staying with friends of the family in Ayrshire.

At first idleness had worried Juliet and she had mentioned her worry to Mrs Crimond. The novelist had looked at her vaguely and then had smiled kindly and told her not to worry.

'Think of this time as a holiday, one which you've needed, dear,' she said. 'Relax, explore the estate, talk to Gareth. He'll be glad of the company. There'll be plenty for you to do later when I've got my story off the ground, and when Maree returns.'

So Juliet had wandered at will about the castle and its grounds and along the shore of the loch. Sometimes Jamie would walk with her and talk about the geology of the area or tell her about caving, but she had the impression that he accompanied her only because his mother had told him to do so. She much preferred the occasional accidental meetings she had with Gareth when he emerged from his study on the ground floor of the wing of the castle, to lounge on the terrace or in the room behind it.

It required only a little shy prompting on her part to make him tell her some of the fascinating legends about the castle and the surrounding district, and she listened attentively, watching the play of expression on his face, her heart full of pity because such a handsome and intelligent person as he was had chosen to become a recluse.

As the days drifted by and he began to realise he had a willing and sympathetic audience, it seemed to her that he did not stay in his room quite so much and that he deliberately sought her out. Every evening at dinner, the only time the family assembled together, he would sit across from her looking at her with deep blue eyes whose expression caused the blood to pound excitedly in her ears as they made her aware for the first time in her life of herself as a woman.

Juliet sighed and stretched luxuriously, and wondered, not for the first time since she had come to Castle Ross, if she were in love. Had love winged, with the darting swiftness of a summer swallow, into her heart at last? How else could she account for this longing to stay there whatever might happen, to help Gareth in any way she could to alleviate the pain and frustration which had been his since the accident which had deprived him of the proper use of his leg?

Gentle and gallant, he fitted exactly her own romantic image of the man whom she could love. If she had ever had any doubts about coming to the castle they had been chased away completely by her growing friendship with him. It had been right for her to come, right for her to meet him. Dared she look further and hope that they might love each other?

Even the arrival of Maree last night could not dispel Juliet's anticipation of another enchanted day, because Maree was part of the enchantment. She was tall for her age with russet-coloured hair and exceptionally clear grey eyes. Maree had shown no signs of the rebelliousness to which Mrs Crimond had referred. Pleased to be back at the castle, she had been happy at dinner, answering her grandmother's questions about her stay in Ayrshire enthusiastically. The friends she had visited apparently owned horses and now Maree wanted nothing more than to own a pony or a horse and to learn to ride.

Yes, thought Juliet, she was looking forward to meeting Maree again this morning. It was most important that she should be friends with Gareth's daughter.

'Miss Grey, are you awake?'

The girl's voice coming from the direction of the door startled her, coming directly as it did after her thought, and she sat up in bed suddenly. Just inside the door, which she must have opened very quietly, stood Maree, her square-shouldered boyish figure dressed in long blue pants and a striped cotton T-shirt. Her short hair stood on end spikily, the result of having pulled the shirt over his head, and under her thick dark eyebrows her eyes were very clear and un-winking.

'You're up early,' said Juliet, as the girl advanced rather shyly into the room.

'Are you really wide awake?' she asked seriously.

'Yes, I am now.'

'I want to show you something. Please will you get dressed and come out with me into the hills?'

'It's very nice of you to ask me, Maree, but before I agree I think I'd better ask your grandmother if she needs me this morning to do some typing for her.'

Maree shook her head slowly from side to side.

'No, she won't. Not in the morning. Anyway, she's not awake yet. There's only you and me and Vinnie awake.'

'Then where is this something you want to show me?'

39

'It's a secret. If you'll get up and get dressed I'll take you to see it.'

As she had already decided that it was important for her to nurture friendship between herself and the girl, Juliet agreed to get up, and having achieved what she wanted Maree grinned happily and slipped out of the room.

Once out of bed Juliet discovered that the morning, although sunny, was cool, so she dressed in jeans and sweater. A peep from the window high up in the wall of the old tower showed her the loch crisp with white-topped waves which had been churned up by the brisk northerly wind, and down in the small bay formed by the curve of the promontory the yacht which belonged to Lance Crimond tossed and tugged at its mooring as if wanting to be free.

In the passage outside her room Juliet found Maree waiting for her and as soon as she appeared the girl slipped a firm hand into hers and led her to the fascinating curved stairway known as a wheel stair which in olden times had been the chief means of access from the main hall of the castle to the storeys above it. The main hall itself had been converted into a small suite of rooms for Mrs Crimond and himself by Robert Crimond, and was shut off from the wheel stair by a stout oak door. Below the suite of rooms on the ground floor the big vaulted store-rooms had been converted into a morning room and an up-to-date kitchen. All the other rooms were in the three-storey wing which, Juliet had learned from Gareth, had been added during the seventeenth century.

Maree took Juliet into the kitchen while Mrs McVinn, who was cook and housekeeper, had already started her day's work. A plump brown-haired woman who moved with brisk confidence about the kitchen, she had impressed Juliet as being a kindly, motherly sort of person. Now she greeted her in her lilting Highland voice,

'You're up early, miss. What would you be liking for your breakfast? The porridge is simmering and then there's ham and eggs, or perhaps you'd like some of the haddock McVinn was after catching last night? Fried in oatmeal they're very good.'

Ever since she had come to Castle Ross Juliet had been trying to avoid eating the heavy breakfasts which Vinnie cooked, but so far she had failed. That didn't stop her from trying again.

'Oh no, just toast and some tea will do. I can get it ready myself.'

'Ach, that's no sort of breakfast for a day like to-day when the wind is fresh. As for getting it ready yourself, that will never do.' Vinnie's sharp black eyes glinted fiercely. 'No one cooks in my kitchen, not even Mrs Crimond. Not that she'd be wanting to. She likes to have her meals prepared fo her, and she likes them on time too.'

'Uncle Lance sometimes cooks in your kitchen,' said Maree. 'When he's been fishing. He says trout have to be cooked as soon as they're caught to taste right.'

'Ach, so he does.' The black eyes softened slightly. 'But then he's the master here now.'

'But he told me he used to get up in the morning before everyone else when he was a boy, even before you, Vinnie, and cook his own breakfast,' argued Maree.

'Aye, and then he'd be away for the rest of the day, a bag of biscuits in his pocket, roaming the hills or sailing his wee dinghy on the loch, and only coming back when it was dark, and not always then. The Lord knows what he did all the time,' said Vinnie. 'And he's no different to-day when he comes here.'

'Daddy says Uncle Lance always likes to live on the edge of danger,' said the informative Maree. 'What does that mean? Do you know, Miss Grey?'

'Please call me Juliet, Maree. I suppose it means that your uncle likes doing things which take him into dangerous places or situations, like climbing hills or sailing.'

'Or caving. That's dangerous too, and Uncle Jamie does that.'

'Aye, and he's another who's never happy unless he's worrying your grannie. Both of them are tarred with the same brush, never giving her a minute's peace. And you're

41

no different, Maree. A madcap, that's what you are.' Vinnie's glance at Maree was wholly affectionate. 'And where are you off to this morning, I'd like to know?'

'It's a secret,' replied Maree coolly.

'You and your secrets!'

'It's all right, Mrs McVinn, I'm going with Maree. I'll see that she doesn't do anything dangerous,' put in Juliet, and Maree flashed her a grateful glance.

The housekeeper looked relieved.

'Then that's just fine,' she said. 'Now away with this blethering. Sit down at the table and I'll be cooking the breakfast I was talking about. Which is it to be? The ham and eggs, or the haddock?'

Once the meal was over Maree lost no time in leading Juliet out of the house into the cool fresh morning air, across the green lawn at the back of the building and straight into the natural woodland of oak and birch which covered the lower parts of the hillside. Through the woods they followed a path which gradually grew steeper and more rocky. Soon they burst out of sweet-smelling sun-shot gloom on to the bare hillside.

Juliet, who by now was out of breath, sat down on an outcrop of rock.

'Let's rest a while, Maree. I'm not used to climbing hills so early in the morning,' she said.

There was a certain amount of scorn in Maree's sidelong glance.

'You're not used to climbing hills at all,' she said bluntly. But she sat down too and together they gazed down at the world spread at their feet; at the squares and oblongs of the castle and its outbuildings; at the swathe of blue water sprinkled with brown rocky islands, widening out to the sea; at the loom of other darker higher islands on the distant horizon.

'Grannie says your mother was a ballet dancer and that you used to work in a ballet school,' said Maree abruptly, 'I think ballet is silly. I'd rather do gymnastics and play games like hockey and basketball, and I'd like to learn to ski, like my mother did.'

'You may think ballet is silly, but you have to be just as physically fit to do it as you have to be to participate in sports. In fact skiing isn't unlike ballet. You can't do either successfully without having exercised properly first,' replied Juliet quietly.

Maree looked at her with a certain amount of respect dawning in her eyes.

'Could you show me how to dance?' she enquired.

'I wasn't a teacher of ballet, only a secretary in Madame Follet's school.'

'But you must know all about it. You must have watched her teaching. You must know the steps.'

'Yes,' admitted Juliet hesitantly, thinking how well she knew them.

'Then you could show me. I must learn everything I can,' said the determined girl. 'Good, that's settled. Come on, we've rested long enough.'

It was astonishing, thought Juliet, as she followed Maree along a sheep path across the shoulder of the hill. Here was the same refusal to take no for an answer, giving her the same feeling that she was being swept along by an irresistible force that she had known when she had first met Lance Crimond. Judging her by her clear grey eyes and her manner Maree might be Lance Crimond's daughter.

Whatever was she thinking? Maree wasn't Lance's daughter. She was Gareth's. Children often resembled uncles or aunts or grandparents more than their own parents. When she looked closely at Maree she would see other characteristics which she had inherited from her mother's family. It was just that on first impression she seemed to be all Crimond.

But instead of having fantastic thoughts she should be watching where Maree was leading her so that she would be able to find her way back to the castle. Looking about her she noticed that the scenery had changed. They were now following the course of a gaily chuckling burn which tumbled over its rocky bed. Ahead the sharp edge of a mountain peered down the glen formed by the burn. Everywhere boulders and stony debris were scattered, and underfoot the grass was short and very green.

As they followed the burn deeper and deeper into the hills, enticed possibly by that sharply outlined mountain, Juliet also noticed a change in atmosphere. Although the burn still chuckled there was something mocking about its laughter, and Juliet, whose imagination was extremely active, had a feeling that if they continued to follow the bubbling water it would lead them to their doom. So strong was this impression that she decided that when she caught up with Maree round the next outcrop of rock she would ask how much farther they had to go before they reached the secret.

But when she eventually rounded the next outcrop of rock the burn disappeared suddenly and dramatically, and all that could be seen was a deep gash in the hillside. Standing near the gash amongst the mass of boulders and scree where the burn had disappeared was Maree, a triumphant grin on her face.

'I found it before I went away to Ayrshire,' she announced. 'This is the place which Uncle Jamie calls the Cauldron and Grannie calls the Hollow Hill. I daren't tell anyone I'd found it because Daddy said I wasn't to go any farther than three miles from the castle. This is really out of bounds for me.'

Completely mystified, Juliet stared at the rough rock of the hillside. The gash or fissure was long and deep and had obviously been made by the fast-flowing water of the burn as it had worn away the rock until it had caved in.

The word *caved* was a clue. This must be the limestone thrust about which Jamie had told her.

'I'd love to go into the crack and see if I can find a way into the passage which leads to the caves under the hill,' Maree went on excitedly. 'It isn't fair of them to keep it to themselves.'

'Them?' queried Juliet, sending her an alarmed glance.

'Uncle Lance and Uncle Jamie. They explored it last

44

summer, but they weren't able to get into the main cave because the passages were too narrow and because there was danger of falling rock. Uncle Jamie wanted to blast, but Uncle Lance wouldn't agree because he was afraid the whole hill might come tumbling down if they did. Uncle Jamie was very disappointed, and I don't blame him. If they'd brought me with them I might have been able to get farther than them because I'm smaller.' Her eyes lit up with a reckless gleam. 'Juliet, do you think that while you're here I could squeeze into the crack and see if I can find the entrance to the passage?'

The edge of danger. Oh, yes, she could see very well what Vinnie had meant when she had said that madcap Maree was every bit as bad as her uncles. Juliet stared at the deep fissure in the rock towards which Maree had pointed and her imagination leapt ahead. Supposing Maree was able to squeeze into the crack and crawl into a passage? Supposing she reached the cave, an echoing place with slippery walls? Supposing she slipped and fell into the rushing water of the underground stream?

Juliet closed her eyes and shook her head. Really, this place was bad for anyone with imagination. She opened her eyes again to find Maree was staring at her.

'Are you all right, Juliet?' she asked sympathetically.

'Yes, I'm fine, thank you, and the answer to your question is no, you are not going to squeeze into any crack while I'm here to watch you. We're going to turn right round and go back to the castle *now*.'

The grey eyes clashed with hers. It was a tense moment for Juliet, a battle of wills which she had to win or she might as well leave Castle Ross immediately. She had to vindicate the trust which she realised, with a slight qualm of uneasiness, had been placed in her by Mrs Crimond. Even at the risk of losing the girl's friendship she had to show her who was in authority.

It was a great effort not to let her gaze waver, but she managed to maintain an outward calm and to outstare the wilful girl. At last Maree lowered her eyes, kicked at a

45

pebble and muttered sulkily,

'All right, I won't. But I thought you'd be a better sport.'

'It's not a question of being a sport, Maree. Surely you're intelligent enough to realise that while you're with me I'm responsible for you, and that your father would never have forbidden you to go this far away from the castle if he didn't have a reason.'

'He thinks it would have been better if I hadn't been born.'

Juliet gasped at the bitterness of the girl's unexpected outburst.

'It's true,' continued Maree. 'I overheard him saying so once to Grannie the time I got lost on the moors and they had to organise a search for me. He doesn't really want me. Nobody has wanted me since Mummy died.'

Juliet's annoyance with the girl faded and died, as the words touched a chord in her memory. How often she had experienced the same feeling of rejection after her parents had died. How often she had reached the edge of despair, only to be rescued by Hilary's kindness and humour.

She touched the girl gently on the shoulder.

'I'm sure that isn't true, Maree. I'm sure there must be somebody who wants you and cares for you. I expect your father does really, and there's your grannie ...'

'She cares only for her silly books!'

'That's not so. I know she cares very much for you and for your uncles too. And both of them must care for you.'

'Uncle Jamie hardly notices me. When I ask him if I can go caving with him he always says I'm too young.'

'And he's probably right, Maree. You are,' said Juliet patiently. 'What about your Uncle Lance? Doesn't he notice you're here?'

'Yes, sometimes. Last summer he took me sailing one day in his boat.' Maree's eyes brightened as a treasured memory was recalled. 'We were gone for the whole day. We landed on one of the islands and had our lunch there. It was a bird sanctuary and Uncle Lance told me all about the

46

birds. He knows about everything. Then we sailed right out to sea.' Her eyes clouded. 'But Daddy spoilt it all. He was awfully cross when we came back. He said Uncle Lance had no right to keep me out so late.'

'Doesn't that show your father cares for you if he was anxious about you?' said Juliet, quick to point out that concern for the safety of his only child had probably been at the root of Gareth's anger.

Maree shook her head slowly.

'No. It's difficult to explain. He wasn't cross because he was worried about me, he was cross because I'd been with Uncle Lance. If I'd been with anyone else he wouldn't have said a word.'

This time Juliet had no argument ready because Maree had touched on a subject which was unknown to her, the relationship between Lance and Gareth. She longed to ask questions, but realised that it wasn't wise or right to pump Maree. Nor should she believe everything Maree told her about her father. The girl's view of Gareth was bound to be coloured by her own overpowering sense of rejection.

'Look, Maree,' she said comfortingly, 'when I was young, younger than you, I lost both my parents in an accident and I had to go and live with relatives. There were many times when I used to feel exactly as you do, that no one wanted me. But I had, and still have, a cousin called Hilary, and when I was down in the dumps she used to tell me not to be silly because she wanted me and needed me, even if it was only to tease me and have a pillow fight with me. And as I grew older I began to realise there's always someone who wants you somewhere.'

'It must be nice to have a cousin,' said Maree. 'Is she older than you?'

'Yes, and she's not long been married to a distant cousin of your father's.'

'Oh! Who is that?' asked Maree, all curiosity. 'Did you go to the wedding? Please tell me about it. I've never been to a wedding.'

Juliet told her about the wedding as they retraced their

steps down the glen and by the time they reached the castle they were on very good terms, having discovered they had a common love of wild flowers and a liking for rolling down grassy banks.

As they approached the castle Jamie came out of the main door and put some cases in the back of his car.

'Hello. Where have you two been?' he asked casually.

'Maree has been showing me the Cauldron and the Hollow Hill,' replied Juliet honestly, having decided that honesty must be her best policy if she had to answer such a question.

He glanced at Maree.

'Oho, mischief, so you found your way there, did you? I might have known you wouldn't rest this summer until you had!' He turned back to Juliet and asked, 'What did you think of it?'

She shuddered, remembering the eerie atmosphere of the place.

'It gave me the creeps,' she admitted.

'I can see your imagination rivals Mother's,' he scoffed. 'But now Maree knows where it is you're going to have your work cut out keeping her away from there. If you don't Lance won't be any too pleased. He's convinced the place isn't safe.'

'Oh, I think Maree has enough sense not to go there and try caving on her own,' replied Juliet calmly, and Jamie's eyebrows shot up in surprise as he glanced again at his niece.

'I hope you're right,' he murmured, 'because Maree has a tendency to do just what she's been told not to do, and remember, caving should never be done without the company of an experienced speleologist like myself or Lance. Now I'm off to Elstone to join the expedition up there.'

'Oh, I wish I could come with you,' cried Maree.

'What would I do with you if you came?' asked Jamie mildly, as he opened the door of his car.

'I could help you. I could get to places where you can't. Oh please, Uncle Jamie, let me come!'

'Another time. When you're older,' he answered carelessly, and getting into the car, he slammed the door shut as if determined to cut off any more appeals. He switched on the ignition, the car started with a roar, gravel chippings spat out from under the wheels as he left at speed, with a grin and a wave of his hand.

'See what I mean?' said Maree almost choking with fury. 'It's always the same. How am I ever going to do everything that Mummy did if no one will take me anywhere and teach me?'

Swinging round, she ran off and disappeared round the side of the house. Juliet hesitated, wondering whether she should go after the girl and talk her out of her frustration. Then reluctantly she decided that this time Maree would have to get over her disappointment alone because Mrs Crimond might be looking for her new secretary.

Entering the house, she paused as she passed the open door of the lounge and looked inside, thinking that perhaps Mrs Crimond might be in there. The room was just as it had been all the other mornings, quiet and sunlit. The French window was open and the curtains swayed in the breeze. Someone must be on the terrace.

As she approached the open window Gareth spoke from the terrace, having seen her coming.

'Good morning, Juliet. I was wondering when I would see you again. Last night when I couldn't sleep for the pain in my leg, I thought of you.'

His unexpected greeting made every nerve in her body tingle and brought a delicate tinge of pink to her cheeks. She sidled through the open window with a sort of diffident eagerness, longing to see him again and yet shy of meeting the very personal gaze of his blue eyes.

He was lounging full length on an upholstered chaise-longue. He was dressed in light fawn trousers and a navy blue casual shirt which was open at the neck. Sunlight glinted on the hairs on his bare forearms and picked out the reddish tints in his thick wavy hair. In one hand he held a book and in the other a pipe, but when he saw her he laid them aside on a table close by.

His lazy glance took in her slight slim figure and she was suddenly aware of how untidy and windblown she must appear after her tramp into the hills, and the pink on her cheeks deepened.

'You were up and out early,' he remarked, 'I saw you leaving with Maree. You mustn't let her make too many demands on you. She possesses a kind of feverish energy and must be going somewhere or doing something all the time. She's very like her mother in that way.'

It was the first time he had ever mentioned his dead wife and Juliet watched an expression of sadness darken his eyes, and once again her soft heart was touched with pity. But when he glanced at her again the sad look had passed.

'Please sit down,' he said, 'and I'll ring for Vinnie and ask her to bring us some coffee.'

'Oh, no!' she blurted quickly. His eyebrows rose in an expression of hauteur and she rushed to explain why she was refusing. 'I must find Mrs Crimond. I'm afraid I'd no idea how far Maree intended to take me. I didn't mean to be so long. I've done nothing for almost three weeks and I'm sure it's time for me to be doing some work. After all, that is why I came here.'

The expression of hauteur was replaced by an expression of indulgent amusement.

'Work? What's that? None of us really works at Castle Ross. It isn't a place which induces one to work. Even Lance relaxes when he comes here. No one is expecting you to work hard, least of all my mother. I expect she's still in her room indulging in her usual form of escapism, pushing her characters around, making them go where she wants, which is something she can't do with her sons. So please be good enough to press the button in the wall over there, and then sit down.'

He broke off abruptly and a frown of frustration marred his handsome face.

'Dammit,' he muttered between clenched teeth, 'I can't even get up and move a chair for you!'

50

His outburst went straight to her heart and the seed of pity already set there and which had begun to grow in that warm and tender environment attained full growth—pity because Gareth, who must have once been quick and active, could no longer perform without difficulty the simple but naturally chivalrous action of placing a chair in a convenient place for a woman.

'Oh, please don't worry about it,' she said. 'I can manage very well, thank you.'

She went across to a basketwork chair which had been set near the balustrade of the terrace.

'Bring it here ... close beside me,' he ordered.

He tried to push the table aside, but it overbalanced and books and papers scattered in all directions.

'Blast!' exploded Gareth, and Juliet set the chair down hurriedly and darted over to pick up the table. Then she went down on her hands and knees to collect the fluttering papers together.

'I suppose I shall get used to being a helpless, useless hulk, one day,' he ground out. Then with a change of tone he added, 'You must forgive me, please.'

The softly spoken request astonished her. Looking up, she discovered he was leaning towards her and that their faces were on a level.

'What is there to forgive?' she whispered.

His eyes widened and their expression changed from despair to intense excitement.

'My impatience and bad temper, my disability,' he murmured.

Mesmerised by the intensity of his gaze, she swayed slightly on her knees as she was shaken by a strong desire to drop the papers and to put her arms round him in an attempt to ease away his bitterness. The papers actually slithered to the floor, unnoticed, and her hands were reaching out when she heard a discreet cough come from the window behind her.

'Were you after needing something?' asked Vinnie.

Brought back to her senses, Juliet half-turned, wondering

51

how much the housekeeper had seen and heard. The bright black eyes were unrevealing and the plump pink face wore a bland and surprisingly servant-like expression. If Vinnie had seen anything she wasn't going to betray her reaction by the flicker of an eyelid.

'Some coffee, please, Vinnie, for Miss Grey and myself,' said Gareth. 'We've just had a little accident. My clumsiness, of course.'

'Of course.' Even Vinnie's voice was devoid of expression as she turned away and was swallowed up into the depths of the lounge.

Juliet bent again to pick up the papers. Then she collected the three books and put them on top of the papers on the table. She picked up the pipe. Hardly had she laid it down than a hand descended on her wrist and still on her knees she was pulled round slightly to face Gareth.

'Juliet, look at me,' he ordered.

She looked up. She was so close to him she could see the flecks of darker blue radiating outwards from the pupils of his eyes.

'Why did you drop the papers?' he asked.

Still troubled by her violent urge to offer comfort to him, she was unable to reply with certainty.

'I'm not sure,' she said, side-stepping the issue. He smiled, and she had an impression that he knew as well as she did why she had dropped them.

'I've been needing someone like you, Juliet, to help me,' he said softly.

A shadow fell across them, blotting out the sun. A voice in which a certain crispness overlaid the Scottish lilt cut sharply across Gareth's softer tones.

'Well, well, you aren't wasting much time, are you, Gareth?'

Juliet snatched her hand out of Gareth's grasp and jumped to her feet. She clasped her arms around her waist in a defensive action while her wide shocked gaze turned to the balustrade, fully expecting to see no one because she believed that she had imagined the shadow and the voice.

But this time he was there in the flesh, wide-shouldered, bold-featured and cold-eyed. He was dressed in a conventional dark suit and a white shirt, clothes which did more to draw attention to his powerful physique and unusual rather saturnine looks than a more colourful style of dress would have done. He must have come up the steps from the garden and approached very quietly.

Having recovered from the start which Lance's sudden appearance had given him, Gareth spoke sharply and rather petulantly.

'Why do you always have to walk so damned quietly?'

'I wasn't walking quietly. You were so intent on making an impression that you didn't hear me,' returned Lance with a grin. His light grey eyes raked over Juliet insolently.

'How are you, Juliet?' he enquired politely. 'Taking to life in the country quite quickly, judging by the leaves and burrs in your hair and the rent in your pants. Have you been walking with Maree?'

Juliet's hands went first to her hair and then to the tear in her pants, but as the meaning of his last question penetrated she stopped feeling to stare at him.

'How do you know?' she asked in an awed voice.

'Maree is the only one here who would take you for a tramp in the woods and possibly even further afield, to a place where a burn disappears underground.'

How did he know? Panic struck at Julie for a moment and she almost turned and fled into the house away from this disturbing man. Then noticing that he was looking at her feet she glanced downwards. Her brown brogues were covered with a film of dust.

She looked up. There was no glint of amusement in the grey eyes. They were ice-cold as they met hers.

'Oh, for heaven's sake, Juliet, sit down,' said Gareth irritably. 'There's no need to stand there dithering because my omniscient brother has guessed you and Maree have been out of bounds this morning. Why are you here anyway, Lance?'

Wishing she could think up some excuse to leave, Juliet

53

sank down slowly on the edge of her chair, her arms once more clasped about her waist as if she were cold. There was no doubt about it, Lance Crimond was a disruptive force who had already irritated Gareth and had made her feel foolish and incompetent.

'Why shouldn't I be here? It's my place.'

His abrupt arrogance was offensive and Gareth was duly offended by it.

'How you love to rub that in, don't you,' he retorted rather wearily. 'If it wasn't for this useless leg of mine I wouldn't stay here. I'd leave now, to-day.'

'Would you?' Lance's voice had a sardonic edge to it. 'Isn't that going a little too far? Where else would you find such comfort and ease without having to lift a finger and without having to pay? No one wishes your leg was better more than I do. But just think of the problems you would have to contend with if it were.'

Juliet gasped audibly. Here was an example of the unkindness Mrs Crimond had told her about. Horrified, she watched Gareth's face contort with anger.

'Shut up, you devil!' he spat at Lance.

'Are you afraid that Juliet will start thinking badly of you? I shouldn't worry. She's very tender-hearted and I expect she's already on your side and hating my guts, aren't you, Juliet?'

The rattle of china being carried heralded the approach of Vinnie with the coffee and saved Juliet from having to make a reply immediately. Contenting herself with what she hoped was a contemptuous glance in Lance's direction, she moved the books and paper on the table to one side so that Vinnie could place the tray on it.

As soon as the housekeeper saw Lance her face lost its bland expression as she smiled warmly at him.

'Ach, 'tis yourself then. And why weren't you after telling me you were coming?'

'I wasn't sure I could get away until late last night. I left Glasgow at five this morning,' said Lance.

'And will you be staying long?'

54

'Ten days, perhaps longer. It depends on business.'

'Heaven forbid,' groaned Gareth, with typical brotherly directness.

'Now that isn't a nice thing to be saying?' said Vinnie, rounding on him. 'He's needing a holiday, I can see that with my own eyes, and what better place is there for him to be having it than here amongst his ain folk?'

'There are times, as you should know, Vinnie, after all these years, when his "ain folk" can do very well without him. And one of them is now,' replied Gareth testily.

To Juliet's surprise Lance laughed.

'A truly brotherly sentiment,' he remarked. 'I know I'm a thorn in your flesh, Gareth. But if I didn't come to prick you now and again you'd soon degenerate into a loathsome mass of frustration and self-pity.'

'Aye, that's so,' said Vinnie, nodding her head and glancing at Gareth with an expression of motherly solicitude in her eyes. 'Shall I be bringing another coffee cup?'

'No, thanks,' replied Lance. 'I'm going up to see Mother in a few minutes. Is Jamie here?'

'Ach, no. He was away to Elstone this morning. 'Tis sorry he will be to have missed you.'

'I may go up there next week-end to see how the expedition is making out.'

Vinnie went away and there was silence on the terrace. Realising that she was expected to pour the coffee, Juliet picked up the coffee pot, her hand shaking a little as she was conscious of Lance watching every move she made.

'I brought a neighbour of ours to her home this morning. She used to be a good friend of yours,' Lance said suddenly to Gareth.

'Oh? Who is she?' Gareth sounded lethargic and indifferent.

'Alison Coates.'

There was another silence, but this time it seemed to Juliet it was loaded with tension.

'And what did she have to say for herself?' Gareth still sounded casual, but Juliet sensed that his indifference was counterfeit.

'Quite a lot. She's just back from working in a hospital in the south of England. She's going to stay at home for a while. Apparently her mother has been ill. She said she'd call in to see us. I suggested she might be able to give you some advice about your leg, and . . .'

'You what?' exploded Gareth irritably. 'Why can't you leave me alone? Why must you be forever suggesting remedies and cures?'

'Alison is a physiotherapist,' said Lance smoothly, as if Gareth hadn't interrupted him. 'She has a great deal of experience in your kind of problem. She might be able to suggest some new exercises.'

'I've had enough of physiotherapy, or any other therapy,' said Gareth forcibly.

Lance shrugged his shoulders.

'O.K., forget it. When she comes over she doesn't have to see you at all, if that's the way you want it.'

The crispness had gone from his voice and it sounded strangely flat and weary. Juliet glanced cautiously at him. He was gazing at Gareth, who was looking down at his coffee as he stirred it. The expression in Lance's eyes surprised her. They were shadowed with anxiety, and she felt an odd tug at her heart. It wasn't pity this time. It was almost a twinge of conscience as if she had been guilty of condemning someone unheard.

Then Lance pushed away from the balustrade and the impression was destroyed. On his way to the house he passed behind her chair and she stiffened involuntarily as she heard him pause. His touch was light on her head as he tried to disentangle a sticky burr from her hair, but even so her scalp tingled in reaction.

'I'd stay and remove the others,' he muttered unexpectedly, 'but I must go and see Mother. Here's a job for you, Gareth. It should keep you occupied for the next quarter of an hour and help you to get even better acquainted with Juliet. But why should I be telling you that? I guess you don't need any advice in that respect. See

56

you later.'

He went as quietly as he had come. Gareth put down his cup and saucer on the table and swore softly under his breath. The expression on his face was withdrawn as if his mind had gone wandering down paths unknown to her.

'I wonder why he's decided to take a holiday now,' he muttered suddenly.

'Most people take a holiday in the summer months,' replied Juliet.

He gave her a kindly but sceptical glance.

'But not Lance. He's not like other people. He does things because he wants to, not because it's the time to do them. He makes his own rules. He'll have some dark and deep reason for wanting to be here just now, and I'm wondering if it has anything to do with Alison Coates. Ah well, only time will tell.' He sighed and moved restlessly. 'Now, what were we talking about when he arrived?' he asked lightly.

'You were saying how much you needed someone to help you,' said Juliet shyly, and pink stained her cheeks again.

'So I was. Now, I know you're here principally to help Mother and to keep an eye on Maree and see that she doesn't get into mischief, but I've been wondering whether you'd also do some typing for me. It would be a great help. I've started to write a book, a political history of Scotland, and . . .'

His voice went on, but Juliet hardly heard. She knew it was silly to feel disappointed, but she couldn't help it. She was sure he hadn't meant he had been needing someone to do typing for him when he'd said he needed help from someone like her. His eyes, his voice, his hand holding hers had conveyed much more than that.

But now his eyes avoided hers, his voice had lost its compelling vibrancy and he made no attempt to take her hand again. She put the blame for his change of attitude on the arrival of Lance and as a result found herself sharing Gareth's feelings regarding his brother's decision to stay at Castle Ross for a few days. She wished Lance Crimond hadn't come. They could do very well without him.

This feeling was increased when she carried the coffee tray into the kitchen a few minutes later and discovered a tearful, subdued Maree eating her lunch at the table.

She had hardly set the tray down on the table when Maree burst out,

'You told Uncle Lance where we went this morning!'

'No, I didn't.'

'Then how did he know?'

'He looked at my shoes and guessed.'

Maree looked at the offending shoes. 'Oh, I see. He would. He knows everything,' she muttered.

'Was he very angry with you for going there?'

'Not thunder and lightning angry like Daddy. He just made me feel mean and small.'

'But how? What did he say?'

'He said I'd deliberately taken advantage of you being new here and not knowing about the Cauldron being out of bounds for me. He said that if he were in your place he wouldn't want to be friends with me because I'd taken advantage of you, but ... but...' Maree's eyes filled with tears and her mouth trembled. 'I didn't mean to take advantage of you, Juliet. You will be my friend, won't you?'

'Of course I will.' Juliet was quick to answer the appeal. She could feel her annoyance with Lance growing. The fact that he had guessed she could be taken advantage of, especially by lonely vulnerable people like Maree, rattled her almost as much as his unkindness to Gareth had aroused her protective instincts.

'And when I ask you to come for a walk with me again you won't think I'm taking advantage of you, will you?' persisted the troubled girl.

'No, I ...' began Juliet, and then stopped as she realised that whenever Maree sought her company in the future she would be a great deal more cautious and would ask a great many more questions concerning their destination before agreeing to go with her. But Maree was staring at her, her grey eyes wide with hurt as she sensed the hesitation. 'I'm sure you aren't going to take advantage of me, are you, Maree?' she went on quickly, touching the girl's hand in a gesture of friendliness. 'Promise?'

They grey eyes blinked once.

'I promise,' muttered the girl. 'Oh, Juliet, I'm so glad you came here.'

At that moment Vinnie came into the kitchen and informed Juliet that Mrs Crimond, who was now having her lunch in her room as usual, expected to see her in half an hour.

'So you'd better be having your lunch quickly and then be changing your clothes and making yourself look tidy instead of sitting there blethering with Maree,' she added sharply.

A little taken aback by the housekeeper's changed attitude, which was indicated by her grimly disapproving glance and her critical words, Juliet ate the meal put before her in silence and then scurried up the wheel stairs to her room.

Truly nothing was as it had seemed at Castle Ross any more, she thought with a regretful sigh as she tried to disentangle burrs from her hair. What a mess she looked, with her hair tangled and her face wind-burnt and her pants torn! So much for behaving like a twelve-year-old and rolling down the hillside. No wonder Mrs McVinn had looked disapproving.

But was her untidy appearance the only reason for the change in the housekeeper's manner? Or had Lance Crimond something to do with that too? Jamie had said Lance had a way of turning up unexpectedly and putting everyone in a tizzy. Well, he'd certainly done that this morning in the short time he'd been here.

Oh, how she wished he hadn't come. For the last three weeks everything had seemed perfect. Castle Ross had seemed an oasis of pleasant gracious living, an impression created not only by the building and its surroundings but also by the highly civilised behaviour of the people living in it. But now she was aware of strange undercurrents of feeling and everyone had changed.

Gareth no longer seemed a quiet gentlemanly person bearing with fortitude the cross of his disability, but had shown he could be peevish and possibly even cowardly in his refusal to go out into the world. Maree no longer seemed to be a lovable madcap whose wildness was due only to lack of attention but had been revealed as capable of taking advantage of others to get her own way. And Vinnie no longer seemed the kindly motherly body to whom nothing was too much trouble but had shown that she could be vindictive and critical of a fellow employee.

It was as if a cold wind had swept through the house whipping away the warm cover behind which everyone had been hiding, and with a shiver Juliet wondered if the wind had reached Mrs Crimond's room too.

It had. Although when she entered the big comfortable room, which Mrs Crimond used as a combined study and private sitting-room, she thought the novelist looked as usual, a leisurely person with plenty of time to stand and stare at a window. But when Mrs Crimond turned to see who had entered the room Juliet could see that her face was creased by lines of worry and that she twined one hand nervously in one of her strings of beads.

'Oh, there you are, Juliet. I've had a most difficult morning. Basil wouldn't behave at all, so I'm afraid I've wasted reams of paper.' She waved a hand in the direction of the floor which was scattered with screwed-up sheets of yellow copy paper.

Juliet knew that Basil was a character in the new book which Mrs Crimond was writing and that he often gave his creator problems. Feeling that she should make herself useful, she moved forward and bent to pick up some of the paper to put it in the waste basket.

'No, don't touch anything, please,' commanded Mrs Crimond. 'You see, dear, there might be the germ of an idea in one of those pieces of paper—which one I can't be sure. Lance says I have no system, and he's quite right. But we can't all be as methodical as he is and I've never been able to work any other way.' She glanced anxiously at Juliet. 'You've seen him, of course.'

'Yes.'

Mrs Crimond swallowed nervously, and once again Juliet felt her annoyance rising as she realised the eldest Crimond had upset his mother as well as everyone else in the house.

'It was too bad of Maree to take you to the Hollow Hill,' murmured Mrs Crimond apologetically. 'And I feel it's my fault for not having warned you. I just didn't think she would do anything like that or that she even knew how to get there.'

'Oh, I do hope Mr Crimond hasn't blamed you for what happened this morning,' Juliet blurted out impulsively.

'Not entirely, but he did suggest that I should have told you more about the area and pointed out the dangers of wandering so far afield. I can see now that it was very thoughtless of me ... if there'd been an accident. Oh, it doesn't bear thinking about!'

'But there wasn't an accident, and we didn't get lost,' said Juliet gently. 'And if Mr Crimond hadn't come this morning he'd never have known that Maree had taken me there and then there wouldn't have been all this fuss about nothing.'

Mrs Crimond regarded her thoughtfully for a moment and then smiled with relief.

'Perhaps you're right, dear, although Lance never makes a fuss, he just has a rather unpleasant way of telling you what he thinks which makes you feel ...'

'Mean and small.'

'That's it exactly. I hope he hasn't been unpleasant to you.'

'Not yet, but Maree told me how he'd made her feel.'

'Well, in a way I'm glad that's how he made her feel because she needs to be put in her place. It was Lance who suggested to Gareth that she should not be allowed to wander at will on the moors, but of course she's very wilful,

61

and very like her mother in that she knows no fear. Moira was a wonderful athlete. She used to go rock climbing, aqua-diving, sailing and skiing and she was as good if not better than many men. In fact, I often used to think she went out of her way to show the opposite sex how much better than they she could be. I remember one year I went with her and Gareth to Chamonix. It wasn't the usual holiday I take at that time of the year, much too cold, but I wanted to get background for a story. I used to watch her come gliding down the slopes leaving poor Gareth far behind. It was while he was trying to catch her that his leg was hurt, and then she had to go skiing alone or with Lance when he came back.'

The blue eyes became vacant and once again Juliet found herself waiting while Mrs Crimond looked into the past. This time she hoped more information about the athletic Moira might be forthcoming, but the clock on the mantelpiece struck the quarter and Mrs Crimond returned to the present.

'Good heavens!' she exclaimed. 'It's time I was leaving. I'm going to drive over to see a neighbour of ours, Janet Coates—Lance tells me she isn't well. Now, I think I've reached the point where you can help me. You can work quite undisturbed up here. I want you to make three copies of chapter one. You'll find there are some alterations scribbled in here and there, but I think you'll understand them all.'

As soon as she was quite sure Juliet had everything she needed in the way of paper and that she understood the intricacies of the old-fashioned typewriter, Mrs Crimond left the room and all was quiet except for the ticking of the clock.

Glad at last to have some work to do, Juliet soon became absorbed in what she was doing and the time slipped by unnoticed as she typed out the opening chapter of the story which contained all the usual touches of suspense one expected in a novel by Tessa Dean.

She had just finished typing chapter one when Mrs

Crimond walked into the room.

'Do you know, dear, it's almost time for dinner. I didn't expect you to work all this time. Always stop at five no matter how much you've done, or Lance will be telling me I'm a slave-driver next. Now, run off and make yourself pretty for dinner. Gareth does enjoy having a pretty girl at the dinner table.'

The mention of Gareth brought back the conversation she had had with him on the terrace that morning, and her heart began to beat excitedly as she started up the wheel stair to the floor above. She was looking forward to seeing him again and seeing his blue eyes light up with appreciation as she entered the dining-room. How good it made her feel to know that he liked the way she looked. It made her want to make an effort with her appearance.

Now, what should she wear? She hadn't much choice really. All the other evenings she had worn alternately a full black skirt and off-the-shoulder gypsy blouse or a simple green summer dress. Dared she wear the sea-green dress she had worn for Hilary's wedding to-night?

'Where do you think you're going?'

Lance's voice startled her. She looked up. He was standing at the top of the stairway, his hand on the curving handrail, in readiness to descend.

'To my room,' she replied stiffly.

'Who gave you a room up here?'

'Mrs Crimond. She said she wanted me to be near her.'

'I see. Well, I suppose that's reasonable enough. I hope you won't mind sharing a bathroom with me.'

'Oh, do you . . .?'

'Yes. In the other room up here. When I was younger I wouldn't let anyone else come up here. I used to consider the whole of this top floor as my eyrie . . .'

'From which you kept an eagle eye on everything.' Strange to think that this cold practical man had indulged in fantasies of that sort.

'How did you guess?' he said, and his lop-sided grin appeared. There were times when he looked very attractive,

63

thought Juliet, and this was one of them. Over an open-necked white shirt he wore a thin charcoal grey sweater which matched his trousers. The white collar of the shirt contrasted sharply with the darkness of his hair and eyebrows and seemed to find reflection in his clear eyes. He had obviously bathed recently, because his hair was damp, sleek as a raven's wing, except for the rebellious lock which slid forward on his forehead.

He leaned a broad shoulder against the whitewashed wall of the stairway, making room for her to pass.

'Aren't you coming up?' he enquired. 'There isn't room for two to pass on these stairs.'

Realising she had been staring at him for some time, Juliet went pink.

'Anyway, it's unlucky to pass on the stairs,' she countered as coolly as she could, and began to mount the steps.

'I might have known you'd be superstitious as well as hopelessly romantic,' he mocked, and as she gained the top stair where he stood he reached out and caught her by the arm so that she was unable to go on. 'Are you sorry you came here?' he demanded.

She glanced deliberately at the hand holding her arm and then tried to move it from his grasp. It was impossible. As at the wedding he had caught her and now he held her with casual ease.

'I haven't been, but I might be now that you've come,' she answered, and felt the hand tighten remorselessly.

'That isn't the sort of thing you should say to your employer, little white rose,' he threatened softly.

The air was cold and sharp in her mouth as she gasped, 'But I thought Mrs Crimond . . .'

'It was my idea for you to come here and work for her and I pay the shot, as I do for everything else around here. And that reminds me, Miss Grey, you slipped up badly this morning, so badly that I'm wondering whether it was a good idea to bring you here at all. You're supposed to keep Maree out of mischief and danger, not lead her into it,'

64

'I didn't lead——' she began, then decided that wasn't the right way to defend herself or Maree, so she added, 'How was I supposed to know the place was dangerous?'

'You weren't to know unless someone told you, and I've already dealt with those who knew for not telling you. Now I realised when I met you that you were a little wet behind the ears, but I didn't realise you were so green as to let a twelve-year-old girl lead you by the nose. Vinnie tells me she tried to find out from Maree where you were going, but you stepped in and said that Maree would be all right with you.'

Silently seething at his insolent taunts, Juliet flung back her head and glared up at him.

'And she *was* all right with me. When I saw the place and she told me that she would like to try and squeeze into the crack in the hillside I wouldn't let her, and I made her come back. I'm not entirely witless and irresponsible.'

'I'm glad to hear it,' he commented dryly. 'But you'll not deny you're very trusting and easily put upon. Children often have a way of finding a person's soft spot. And you're soft, aren't you, Juliet? Soft and tender-hearted, and already a little bit in love with Gareth.'

He had dealt with the others and now he was dealing with her, punishing her with a series of taunts. He wasn't angry. She would have preferred anger to this cold approach which like the cold wind penetrated into the most protected parts of her heart so that now she hated him for having noticed how she felt about Gareth.

'Since you find me so unsuitable perhaps you would like me to leave?' she said shakily, and was mortified when he merely grinned at her.

'Not so fast,' he murmured. 'I didn't say you were unsuitable. I was only exercising my prerogative as an employer to see that I'm getting value for my money. You might be interested to know that when I learned you were looking for a job I couldn't help thinking how suitable you would be to fill the need here and how good you'd be, not only as a secretary to Tess and a companion for Maree, but also how you might be able to help Gareth, I'm still of that opinion. The accident in which his leg was hurt coupled with the unexpected death of his wife damaged his self-esteem and went a long way to making a recluse of him. He needs someone to make a fuss of him. You were doing pretty well this morning on the terrace, so I've no criticism on that score.'

To her consternation Juliet's face flamed, and she couldn't meet his eyes.

'But on the subject of Maree I think perhaps you need a little guidance,' he continued. 'She doesn't need yet another person over whom she can ride roughshod. She's done that already to Tess, and to Vinnie. As a result she has little or no respect for them and they have no control over her. Gareth only stirs himself occasionally to berate her and then sinks back into his lethargy. Her wilfulness could lead one day to an accident, and there have been enough accidents in this family recently. Do you understand?'

'But why should you be concerned about her? She isn't your child,' she said, looking up at him. His eyes were cold and crystal clear as the burn she had followed that morning and they gave no indication of his feelings.

'Everyone living here is my concern in some way or other,' he replied quietly, and once again she felt that strange twinge of conscience as if she had been guilty of prejudice.

'Because you pay the shot?' She couldn't resist flicking the barb and should have known he would react unpredictably. Instead of retaliating he laughed and released her arm.

'You can think of it that way if you wish, it makes no difference to me,' he murmured, and watched her rubbing the place where he had held her arm. 'That's all I have to say for the time being, and unless you make another mistake you'll hear no more criticism from me. Do what you came here to do—type for Tess, take an interest in Maree so that she has no reason to wander and throw in some attention for Gareth by way of good measure and you'll

66

earn every penny of your wages and I think you'll find life quite pleasant. But,' he paused as if to add emphasis to what he was going to say, 'anything beyond those duties is not your concern. Do I make myself clear?'

Juliet nodded. He meant that she wasn't to step beyond the limits he had just imposed and get involved with anyone else other than the three people he had just mentioned, and it wasn't until he had gone down the stairs that she realised she had just received a warning to keep her nose out of Crimond family affairs.

CHAPTER THREE

WHEN Juliet reached her bedroom she found she was trembling. If every meeting with Lance Crimond was going to do this to her, she thought with a wry smile, she would be a nervous wreck by the end of his ten-day holiday. And as if his presence in the castle wasn't enough, he had to have his bedroom on the same floor as hers, right across the passage. At night they would be the only two up here in the eyrie to which he wouldn't allow anyone else to come when he was a boy. However was she going to sleep knowing he was there? The very thought made her shudder again.

His remarks about herself and Gareth had destroyed the zest with which she had been looking forward to dressing for dinner. She dressed absentmindedly, automatically putting on the black skirt and gypsy blouse, her eyes avoiding the sea-green dress which Lance had once told her made her look elegant and mysterious, her subconscious instinctively drawing back from anything which had associations with him. She made no attempt to arrange her hair differently as had been her intention, but after brushing it let it hang loosely to her shoulders.

But by the time she took her place at the table in the dining-room her poise had returned, restored by Gareth's warm greeting as she had entered the room and the pleasure which lit his eyes as they lingered appreciatively on her slim waist accentuated by the broad band of the skirt, and on her white-skinned throat and shoulders as revealed by the wide scooped neckline of the blouse.

Maree, her hair brushed until it shone, wearing a blue and white striped knit dress whose short skirt revealed her sturdy tanned legs, sat down next to Juliet and Lance took his place at the head of the table facing Mrs Crimond.

As on previous evenings Mrs Crimond and Gareth carried on a light and stimulating conversation designed, Juliet was sure, to inform herself and Maree on all manner of subjects and to give them both a chance to participate. Lance contributed nothing, but occasionally his bright observant glance would flick from one face to another, and Juliet had the impression that he didn't miss one word that was said. Certainly she found his presence at the table a restraint, causing her to choose her own words with care when she had something to say, so it was with a feeling of relief that she saw him toss his table napkin down when he had finished his dessert, and rise to his feet with a muttered excuse.

'Oh, Uncle Lance, are you going fishing? May I come with you, please?' pleaded Maree impulsively, also rising to her feet, obviously just as eager to leave the table as he was.

'Not this evening. I have something else to do,' he replied, his smile glimmering briefly as he turned in the doorway. 'But if you can be up early in the morning and ready about six o'clock you could come with me then. I'm going to fish the Black Pool. McVinn tells me that the trout offer a good fight up there.'

'I'll be up,' answered the girl, her eyes flashing with excitement.

'Maree, you will do nothing of the sort,' said Gareth curtly. 'You are not to go fishing with Lance.'

Lance flicked a cold but slightly derisive glance at his brother.

'Juliet could come too to act as watchdog if you're worried in case something might happen to Maree while she's with me. She took good care of her to-day,' he said quietly.

The atmosphere in the room twanged with tension. Mrs. Crimond's left hand began to twine nervously in one of her necklaces. Gareth's eyes darkened and his mouth went taut as he tried to control his easily roused temper.

Aware of antagonism between the two brothers, Juliet felt rebellion rising within her. Nothing, not even the threat of the sack, would make her go with Lance to-morrow, just to look after Maree. She looked across at Gareth hoping he would continue to refuse to allow Maree to go fishing with her uncle.

'I'm sure Gareth isn't thinking that anything might happen to Maree while she's with you,' protested Mrs Crimond nervously.

'And I'm sure that he is,' said Lance. 'Well, Gareth? Will you let her come if Juliet comes too?'

In answer to the question in Gareth's eyes Juliet shook her head slowly, trying to make the action as imperceptible as possible, hoping that Lance wouldn't see it.

'As a matter of fact I was hoping Juliet would be available to do some typing for me in the morning,' said Gareth lightly. His gaze was steady as it met Juliet's and she smiled her thanks. In return she received a warm sympathetic smile.

'Wonders will never cease,' jibed the hateful man in the doorway. 'I wouldn't want to be responsible for coming between you and work, Gareth, so of course Juliet must stay. Sorry, Maree. Your luck's out this time. Try another day.'

He went out of the room. The tension snapped as Maree turned on her father with a howl of disappointment.

'Why will you never let me go with him? Why? Why?' she raged. 'He's the only one who ever wants to take me anywhere, and you'll never let me go. Why?'

Seeing tears brim in the girl's eyes, Juliet felt suddenly guilty. After all, she was here to take an interest in Maree. That had been the second on her list of duties which her employer had enumerated on the wheel stairs less than an hour ago, and helping Gareth had been only third. Perhaps she should have made an attempt to show she was willing to go fishing so that the girl could go too. If the fisherman had been anyone other than Lance, she would have done so, she argued with herself, but the thought of having to spend a whole morning, possibly a whole day, in his company, frightened her.

'Maree, you're behaving in the most ridiculous manner,' said Gareth sharply. 'I just don't want you to go, and that's reason enough.'

'It's because of Mummy, isn't it?' shrilled the girl. 'It's because she was with Uncle Lance when she was killed, isn't it?'

Gareth and Mrs Crimond spoke together, one ordering the girl to go to her bedroom and stay there until she could behave herself, and the other remonstrating with more gentleness and suggesting that Maree didn't know what she was talking about. At that moment Vinnie entered the room to say she had put the coffee tray in the lounge and to comment that it was a fine evening and that the wind had gone down at last. She clucked her tongue at the sobbing girl, put an arm round her and said in the motherly way which had impressed Juliet when she'd first met her,

'There, there, bairn, what's the good of carrying on like this? You'll only exhaust yourself. McVinn will take you fishing this evening on the loch.' She looked over the girl's head at Gareth. 'You'll be letting her go with him?'

Gareth assented rather wearily and Maree went with Vinnie willingly. With a sigh of relief Mrs Crimond stood up and drifted out of the room. Gareth attempted to rise to his feet, only to subside into his chair again, a rather bitter expression on his face. Pity turning like a knife in her heart, Juliet hurried round to his side.

'Can I help?' she asked.

His smile was rueful.

'I'm afraid it's one of those days when my leg seems remarkably useless. I'll try again.'

This time he managed to stand, but when he moved forward at her side he placed his free hand on her shoulder as if seeking support. Under his touch the half bare skin seemed to burn.

'You're very understanding, Juliet,' he murmured as they went out into the hallway.

'I could say the same for you. I ... I didn't want to go fishing,' she stammered truthfully, 'but now I'm wondering whether I should have said I'd go for Maree's sake.'

'Nonsense. She can go fishing any time with McVinn. She doesn't have to go with Lance.'

'But she must be feeling very disappointed and miserable.'

'It's her own fault. She shouldn't behave so badly.'

'She's only a child...'

'I know, and I'm a rotten father because I don't take sufficient interest in her and in what she wants to do. But how can I when all she's interested in is climbing hills, fishing, sailing, exploring underground caves, and I can't do any of those things any more?'

'Did you ever do them?'

His grin was a little self-disparaging.

'Not much. I'm not really the outdoor type. I used to ski a little to try and keep up with Moira.'

'What's wrong with your leg?'

'It's apparently paralysed, something to do with pressure on a nerve.'

'Isn't it possible to have an operation?'

'All avenues have been explored in that direction and I've been told that nothing can be done,' he replied curtly. 'Some days it seems better than others. Some days like today it seems to stiffen up completely.'

His voice was cool, setting her at a distance, making it obvious that he didn't like to discuss his leg, and she was quick to respond.

'I'm sorry, Gareth,' she murmured. 'So terribly sorry.'

His eyes crinkled at the corners as he smiled at her.

'I meant it when I said that I wanted you to type for me

to-morrow morning,' he said. 'It wasn't just an excuse to get you out of going with Lance, although I realise that what I want wouldn't weigh with him if he insisted that you go. He calls the tune around here.'

'So I'd noticed,' said Juliet dryly, remembering her recent interview on the wheel stair. 'But is it necessary always for you to dance?'

He gave her a surprised glance.

'No, it isn't, but it takes a lot of effort to defy him ... and then he makes it difficult because he's so damned generous. Sometimes I think that perhaps he's trying to make amends for what happened, but I don't know, I just don't know.' He smiled down at her. 'But you don't want to be burdened by our family problems. Let's go out on the terrace while there's still light in the sky.'

Longing to know more but very conscious still of the warning Lance had given her on the stairs about anything beyond her work being none of her concern, Juliet suppressed the questions which clamoured to be asked and went with Gareth through the shadowy lounge out on to the terrace where Mrs Crimond had taken the coffee tray.

The evening was still and tranquil and above the opposite hills the pale green sky was streaked with rose-tinted feathery clouds of which the colours were reflected in the smooth loch below.

'Do you like your coffee black or white, Juliet?' asked Mrs Crimond. 'I'm afraid I've forgotten already. White? Sugar too? Yes, I'm really becoming very forgetful these days. Even Janet noticed this afternoon. Poor dear, she's not been at all well—a slight heart attack. I'm not surprised. How often have I told her that she rushes around too much? Now she has to rest. That's why Alison is home, Gareth. And such a change in her. She's quite sophisticated, although underneath I'm sure she's still the good-natured girl we all used to love.'

'Did we?' Gareth raised his eyebrows haughtily. 'I seem to remember loathing her because her hair was so red and she had a temper to match it.'

'Oh, not loathe, Gareth, surely?' chided Mrs Crimond absently, as she placed his coffee beside him. 'Anyway, I think Lance has gone over to Glenavon to see her this evening. He and Alison have been meeting in Glasgow quite frequently.'

'Have they now? That's interesting,' murmured Gareth.

'Isn't it?' crowed Mrs Crimond, who was obviously delighted. 'Both Janet and I think we can hear wedding bells at last. I'm so glad Lance is showing an interest in a woman and that she's someone with a similar background who would fit into the family perfectly.'

Gareth moved his good leg restlessly and crossed it over his stiff one.

'Mother, stop being naïve. Lance has always shown an interest in women. Wasn't there some talk of Alison being engaged to a surgeon? If she's broken off her engagement in favour of Lance ten to one he'll lose interest in her and go off hunting in some other direction.'

'That isn't a very nice thing to say about him,' remonstrated Mrs Crimond, and the shadow of anxiety was back in her face. 'You'll shock Juliet, and she'll think he's only interested in women who are already engaged.'

'Or married,' put in Gareth bitterly. 'I'm prepared to bet Juliet knows a few things about Lance that aren't nice already. It may not be nice, but it's near the truth, Mother, as you should know.'

Mrs Crimond's hand twined in her necklaces.

'You're thinking of Moira,' she said, 'but I'm sure he was only trying to help both you and her, in his own way. You know how frustrated she was after your injury. I think Lance thought he was helping by taking her out of your way for a few hours.'

'Sometimes it was days,' growled Gareth.

'Oh, surely not!'

'That time they went up to Aviemore and said they couldn't get back because they were snowbound in one of the lodges, they were away three whole days together.'

'But there were other people stranded with them,' objected Mrs Crimond.

'So Lance said,' replied Gareth, with a cynicism which surprised Juliet. 'I often think that if I hadn't let her go with him that last time she might have been alive now,' he added in a low voice, and Mrs Crimond looked startled.

'Now, dear, it doesn't do to keep brooding about it,' she said soothingly. 'If you don't mind I'll leave you because I've had an idea about Basil. I must go and write it down before I forget it. I'll see you to-morrow, Juliet. You type beautifully, by the way, and you seem to have deciphered my squiggles very well. I think Gareth is going to find you a great help to him in his work.'

'I know I am,' murmured Gareth, smiling at Juliet as his mother went into the house, and Juliet, whose thoughts were a little chaotic after the recent interchange between mother and son which had shed an entirely new light on that unknown quantity called Lance Crimond, stood up and walked over to the balustrade to gaze at the rose-tinted water of the loch, shimmering beween dark hills. She could see a lone rowing boat in which two people were sitting silhouetted against the sky and water and beyond the boat on the distant horizon a light flickered in and out at regular intervals. She supposed it was a beacon or lighthouse on a far-off shore and was fascinated by the fact that though she could see the light no land was visible. When she looked in the other direction several lights twinkled at her from the houses of the village which curved round the head of the loch.

'Has your mother ever had a secretary before?' she asked, putting into words at last the problem which had been in her mind ever since she had started typing that afternoon.

'Once. A Miss Reid, but she didn't last long. She couldn't stand Mother's vagueness. Why do you ask?' said Gareth lazily.

Juliet turned and leaned back against the balustrade. Gareth was lighting his pipe and the smell of tobacco wafted towards her, pungent in the soft clear evening air.

'I'm trying to find out why I've been taken on as her secretary. She doesn't need anyone to type her stories for her. She's a perfectly good typist herself.'

Having got his pipe going Gareth removed it from his mouth and stared at her as he considered her statement.

'Don't you like being here?' he asked.

'Oh, yes, I like being here very much, only ...'

'Only someone has disturbed you to-day and started you off questioning motives,' he suggested softly. 'I should leave well alone if I were you, Juliet. Although my mother doesn't need a typist as such, she does need help in other ways. She gets very tired and bewildered sometimes. She hasn't a daughter, and I think she regrets the fact that she hasn't a daughter-in-law. You noticed, I expect, her delight at the thought that Lance at last might be serious about Alison.' He paused and took a puff at his pipe, then added more lightly, 'And if you think you haven't enough to do just wait until to-morrow morning. Mother may be a good typist, but I am not, and I need your help very much. So stop questioning Juliet and be glad you're here, and for goodness' sake don't let him frighten you away.'

'Him?' she queried.

'Lance. He'll only be here for ten days, two weeks at the most, and when he's gone everything will be as it was before he came.'

Before she went to bed that night Juliet went to the kitchen to make her peace with Vinnie. She realised that if she was going to be comfortable during her stay at Castle Ross she must be on good terms with the housekeeper. Being of a gentle disposition she was quite ready to admit that it was her fault that Vinnie had been hauled over the coals by Lance Crimond that morning.

'Ach, don't be worrying your head about that,' said the black-eyed woman. 'I'm used to being told my place by himself, and I'd think less of him if he didn't do it. He was right. I should have warned you about how easy it is to get lost on these moors and about the Cauldron. But you seemed so confident this morning it didn't seem necessary.'

Yet for all the housekeeper's apparently good-natured dismissal of the incident Juliet was still conscious of the woman's withdrawal, and was sure that Vinnie disapproved of something which she had done that day. Even a close analysis of the day's events while she lay sleepless in bed later gave her no clue as to what she had done to earn disapproval.

Suddenly exhausted, she turned on her side and closed her eyes. All the other nights she had slept soundly, dreamlessly, lulled into a sense of security by the smooth effortless rhythm of life at the castle. But to-day that rhythm had been broken by the arrival of one man.

A board creaked in the silence of the night and she shot up in bed, quivering. Her straining ears caught the sound of a door knob being turned quietly. It was followed by the sound of water running through pipes. She relaxed on her pillows and tried to quell the frightened pounding of her heart. She had forgotten that Lance's bedroom was opposite hers and that he would be using the same bathroom.

He must have returned from his visit to see the red-hiared Alison whom he had been meeting frequently in Glasgow and whom Mrs Crimond hoped he might marry. Her mind drifted on, recalling the rest of the conversation between Gareth and his mother concerning Lance's association with Moira, Gareth's wife, and Gareth's low-voiced regret that he let Moira go with Lance that last time.

She turned again and punched her pillow to make it more comfortable. Whatever was the matter with her? She must keep her curiosity under control and not allow herself to be swayed by chance remarks about her employer. She must remember that although she had her doubts about the job she had been offered to do here, she was being paid to type for Mrs Crimond, who didn't need a typist, take an interest in Maree, and give some attention to Gareth. Anything beyond that was not her concern and that 'anything' presumably included Lance's relationship with his late sister-in-law.

In the week that followed his arrival she found it easy to do what Lance had said she should do, and gradually a routine developed, although she could never have complained of being overworked.

Every morning she typed for Gareth and listened to his pleasant voice as he dictated information he had unearthed about the family which had built Castle Ross and which had played a prominent part in the rather chaotic political scene at the time of Mary, Queen of Scots. From his mother he had inherited an ability to tell a story, and this, added to his meticulous attention to historical fact, brought the past vividly alive.

In the afternoon she transferred from fact to fiction as with Basil and Anita she tried to unravel the secret of an old house set in the middle of a bleak and windy moor somewhere in Scotland.

When she wasn't required by either Mrs Crimond or Gareth she showed Maree how to exercise for ballet or went walking along the loch shore with her. By unspoken mutual agreement they kept away from the hills and the moors, although there were days when the sun shone out of a cloudless sky and every summit of every mountain was revealed and Juliet felt the pull of those distant places. On such days, too, she would feel the pull of the sea which heaved and glinted at the mouth of the loch as she watched Lance's boat apparently flying over the foam, its white sails translucent in the sunshine.

To her relief she saw little of her employer, a circumstance which pleased her because it meant she didn't have to take much avoiding action, since she had decided that the less she saw of him during his holiday the more she was likely to keep her employment there. If he wasn't sailing he was fishing, and if he wasn't doing either of those things she presumed he was visiting Alison.

But if she saw little of him, she heard him a great deal, for every morning between the hours of six and seven she would be awakened by his powerful baritone voice as he sang to himself in the bathroom. The first time she heard him she had not believed it was he who was singing but had thought he had a record player in his room upon which he was inconsiderate enough to play records early in the morning. But as she was just considering remonstrating with him the song had stopped in the middle and for a while all that she had heard was the swishing of water, followed by a rather muffled rendering of a different song of which he apparently didn't know all the words, because the singing gave way to humming and whistling before he went out of the bathroom and returned to his bedroom.

She supposed she would get used to it eventually, she thought, on the seventh day of waking early. Turning over lazily, she considered dreamily this unusual aspect of the domineering man who had bullied her into meeting his mother and as a result of that meeting in coming to Castle Ross.

The songs he sang were a mixture of British and American folk songs, many of which she had learned herself at school, with the occasional modern ballad thrown in. Sometimes he even attempted an operatic aria. To sing with such light-hearted abandon at that hour of the morning he must be a truly happy man. But then, when she thought about it, hadn't he everything to make a man happy? He was wealthy, he owned a beautiful castle on a fine estate, and it looked as if he was about to marry the lovely Alison Coates.

For Alison Coates was lovely, with that fine-boned fine-skinned beauty which so many Scottish women seemed to possess. Her hair glowed like beech leaves in the autumn and her eyes were the colour of topazes. Juliet had met her only once, on the previous day, when Alison had called to see Mrs Crimond. She had arrived on an old bicycle which she had thrown down on the drive before coming in by way of the kitchen. Vinnie had greeted her as if she had been the long-lost daughter of the house and Alsison had gone through and up the wheel stair as if sure of welcome.

'Who's that?' Maree had demanded.

'Miss Alison Coates,' Vinnie had replied.

'Oh, she's Aunty Janet's daughter. I've never seen her before.'

'She hasn't been here for a long time, more's the pity,' Vinnie had said, with one of her disconcertingly vindictive glances at Juliet.

'She's pretty,' Maree had remarked. 'I'm going to wait here until she comes down from Grannie's room so that I can see her again. Will you tell her who I am, Vinnie?'

'Well, now that'll be depending on how you're behaving.'

Alison's visit to Mrs Crimond lasted no more than half an hour and when she had appeared again in the kitchen she had gone straight up to Juliet and had held out her hand.

'You must be Juliet Grey,' she had said in her forthright way. 'Tess said I was to send you to her at once. I'm afraid I've prevented you from getting on with your work, but I had to give her a message from my mother.'

She had looked then at the girl sitting beside Juliet and had smiled down at her,

'And you must be Maree. I've been hearing all about you from your grannie. How would you like to come back with me to Glenavon? Have you a bicycle?'

No one could expect the girl to resist the warmth of Alison's approach, thought Juliet, as she turned restlessly on her bed. She couldn't herself. Everything about Alison proclaimed her to be generous, outgoing, strong and competent, and one day she would be the wife of Lance Crimond.

Deciding suddenly that she could lie in bed no longer, Juliet flung back the covers and searched for her slippers. No noise from the bathroom indicated that Lance had finished washing. Taking her dressing gown from the wardrobe, she slipped it round her shoulders and snatching up her toilet bag from the dressing table, she opened the door and stepped out into the passage just as Lance stepped out of his room.

'Oh!' gasped Juliet in surprise, pulling her dressing gown around her and backing into her room.

'Good morning,' he said calmly. 'You're up early.' He

closed his door and leaned against it as if he had all the time in the world to stand and talk. 'Couldn't you sleep?' he added.

'I defy anyone to sleep when someone is roaring out the Soldiers' Chorus from *Faust* in the next room!' she snapped crossly.

'I'm complimented to know that it was actually recognisable,' he returned imperturbably, his eyes busy noting the two plaits of hair which hung on either side of her face, the frill at the neck of her Victorian-styled nightdress, the line of her limbs showing through its flimsy material, the pale dancer's feet in the mules peeping below and then coming back to her face.

'What do you intend to do to-day?' he asked abruptly.

'To-day?' she was puzzled.

'It's Saturday. Had you forgotten? I'm not such a grim taskmaster that I expect you to type your fingers to the bone all day and every day. You are entitled to have the week-end off, you know.'

She had forgotten it was Saturday. On other Saturdays she had walked to the village and back and on Sundays she had gone to church with Vinnie.

'I hadn't made any plans,' she replied.

'The wind's in the west and I'd thought of sailing up north as far as Oban. I'll be leaving in about three-quarters of an hour. You're welcome to come with me if you'd like to. You'd get a different view of the land and see some of the islands.'

The invitation was so unexpected and answered such a deeply-felt desire that she was silent for a few seconds.

'Could Maree come with us?' she managed to say at last, knowing how much the girl longed to go sailing again.

'I believe there is already something laid on for her entertainment, to-day. She's going visiting with Tess and Gareth,' he replied smoothly. 'Anyway, think about it while you're dressing and let me know if you want to come when you come down for breakfast.'

Juliet thought about it, not clearly and concisely, but in a state of turmoil. Her first muddled thoughts, which were dictated not only by her dislike of Lance but also by convention, urged her to refuse. But her second equally muddled thoughts were more adventurous and liberal. How many times had she wished recently that she could board a sailing boat and skim over the water under billowing sails to those enticing islands. The opportunity to go had been offered and it might not come her way again. There was no one to frown and tell her she shouldn't go. Perhaps this was a case when second thoughts should be followed and let the devil take the consequences.

Quickly, before she could change her mind, she dressed in slacks, shirt and sweater and rubber-soled canvas shoes. When she entered the kitchen she found Lance alone at the table eating his breakfast and reading the previous day's newspaper which he had propped against the tea-pot. His quick all-seeing glance flicked over her.

'I take it you've decided to come, he murmured. 'Your breakfast is in the oven keeping warm.'

There was no sign of Vinnie. The kitchen was quiet and sunlit. Lance continued to read the newspaper, moving it only to pour some tea for her. How odd, she thought, to be sitting here with a man I dislike, eating the breakfast he must have cooked for me. Then the domestic intimacy of the scene struck her. Anyone coming in unexpectedly would think that she and Lance had been taking their breakfast together like this for years, like a married couple, so in tune that they didn't have to speak to each other.

'It makes fantastic reading,' drawled Lance, and she jumped. Looking up, she encountered his eyes above the edge of the newspaper. How cold and clear they were, icy pools fringed with black.

'W-What does?' she stammered, fully expecting him to quote from some article in the paper.

'Your face. Would you like to be married?'

She had forgotten his magical ability to read the expressions on her face. She would really have to be more careful in guarding her thoughts from him.

'Not to you,' she retorted, hoping to put an end to such personal probing, and then was immediately surprised by the little leap of pleasure she felt when his rare and unexpected smile appeared.

'Point conceded,' he said good-humouredly. 'But remember you're the next to marry in your family. You caught the bouquet. Would Gareth suit, do you think?'

Rather bewildered by his question, she stared at him trying to guess what lay behind it, but no matter how she stared he remained unperturbed, returning her wide-eyed gaze steadily.

'I haven't known him very long, so I can't tell you,' she replied eventually.

'You surprise me,' he mocked. 'I thought it was a case of love at first sight. But you do find him attractive even though he has a gammy leg, hasn't a job and at the moment is wholly dependent on his allowance out of my father's estate?'

'A man doesn't have to be sound in limb, or fully employed, to be attractive. Gareth has a gentle, kindly disposition as well as a very fine intellect. Who could help but like him?' she said gravely.

'Do you know, that's exactly what I thought you'd say, little white rose,' he remarked with a touch of dryness. 'Now, if you've finished your breakfast you'd better go and fetch a warm jacket, if you have one. Sometimes it can be cool on the water and we may not get back until late tonight.'

Her doubts about him aroused by his recent remarks, Juliet hesitated as first thoughts came crowding back. Perhaps she shouldn't go sailing with him after all.

'Oh, but I don't think ... I mean, do you think we should stay out late?' she stuttered as confusion reigned in her mind once more. His sardonic glance made her feel even more confused.

'One of the most exciting parts of going sailing is not knowing what will happen on the way or when I arrive at my destination, and also in not knowing whether I'll be coming back the same day. It's the not knowing which makes it exciting,' he replied, and as she met the challenge in his eyes she felt a faint flicker of affinity with him. But convention had to have its last fling.

'Won't Mrs Crimond wonder where I've gone?'

'I'll leave a note with Vinnie. She'll tell her. And now unless you've changed your mind, go and get that jacket and meet me down at the boat house.'

Lance's boat wasn't big by yachting standards, so he told her. It was small enough for him to handle alone, and was sturdy enough to stand up to the rough weather often encountered amongst the Hebridean Islands. He had bought it to provide himself with a sure means of escape when he had realised the weight of responsibility he had inherited when his father had died.

'Sometimes I think the old man left me a heavy load as a way of punishing me for the trouble I caused him when I was younger,' he told Juliet, with a laugh.

'But wouldn't coming to stay in Castle Ross be escape enough?' she asked innocently, a little surprised by his confession. The boat heeled suddenly as it moved forward out of the shelter of the bay in which it was usually moored, and into the open water of the loch where the wind was fresh. Feeling a little apprehensive at the sight of the water creaming along the side of the boat so close to the deck, she leaned back against the cockpit coaming and braced her feet against the opposite seat to prevent herself from sliding forward.

'No, it's only part of the load,' said Lance crisply. 'I don't enjoy being my brother's keeper or acting as my mother's treasurer. There was a time in my life when I wanted to live at Castle Ross all the time, but now...' He broke off and shrugged. 'Enough of problems. We've come sailing to forget them, and as soon as we've cleared the entrance to the loch I'm going to give you your first sailing lesson. Meantime you can help with the jib when we have to tack, by freeing that rope over there and then pulling this one in on this side, when we've gone about.'

When eventually he decided to go about Juliet did her best to obey his orders but managed to get the rope she freed fouled round the mast so that she couldn't pull in the rope on the other side. Leaving her to hold the tiller, Lance went forward to free the fouled rope. Filled with trepidation, she hung on to the wooden tiller, not sure what to do. The swish of the water around the hull, the loud cracking sound of the sails, the flick of her own hair pulled out of its ribbon by the tormenting wind, against her face and eyes, all unnerved her. For a few minutes everything seemed out of control.

Then Lance freed the rope and he was back in the cockpit pulling in on the other rope with jerks of his big shoulders. The boat heeled violently and water cascaded into the cockpit. The tiller was snatched from her hand and she was shoved roughly out of the way, the boat steadied as the rail came out of the water, and surged forward again.

Juliet rubbed the funnybone in her elbow which she had banged against the edge of the cockpit when she had been pushed aside and gave Lance an alarmed glance. His grin was a white slash and his eyes glittered like diamonds.

'Did you get bruised?' he asked. 'I'd forgotten you're a sensitive plant unused to the rough and tumble of outdoor life. If I hadn't pushed you out of the way we might have taken more water over the side.'

She could tell by his grin and the glitter of his eyes that he had enjoyed the brush with danger and was pleased that he had been equal to dealing with it, and she suddenly understood why he liked sailing or any other activity with an edge of danger to it. He was much more suited to dealing with crisis situations when he was sailing or caving or even working on a construction site than he was to sitting in an executive's office or lounging on the terrace at Castle Ross. As his mother had once said, he was principally a man of action and not of words.

He hadn't cared about her being bruised or about her being scared silly by the contortions of the boat when she had held the tiller. In her imaginary sail down the loch the boat had skimmed over the water smoothly and silently with none of the jerking, plunging motion which was now threatening to bring up her breakfast.

But she mustn't be sea-sick, not yet, when she'd only been on the boat about half an hour, and certainly not in front of this tough self-contained man who hadn't an atom of chivalry in his character, and who had definitely been miscalled Lancelot!

So she swallowed her nausea and indignation, and hanging grimly with both hands to the side of the cockpit she turned her face to the bow of the boat, which chose that moment to plunge down into a deeper than normal trough in the waves and to rise up again sharply, sending a cascade of spray slap into her face.

Hair drenched and face dripping, she turned to splutter her objections to Lance and was immediately irritated to find that he was sitting completely relaxed, watching the mainsail. He was dry except for a sprinkling of water on his hair and she realised that she had sheltered him from the worst of the spray.

His gaze came down from the sail to her face and he made no attempt to hide his amusement at her appearance.

'There's a towel down below, and an oilskin jacket and sou'wester. You might find them all useful,' he suggested.

She turned and looked at the hatchway. Like the rest of the boat it was tilted at an angle. To reach it she would have to leave her present fairly secure position and start on a perilous journey on which she might suffer more bruises. Then she would have to negotiate the steps down into the cabin, and once there ... Juliet's stomach heaved slightly as she imagined the movement down there. She couldn't go. She would have to stay wet. She looked quickly once more in the direction of the bow and received another salty slap in the face which left her gasping.

'Never mind,' comforted Lance. 'There won't be much more of this. It's the westerly wind which has caused this violent swell in the loch. Once we're clear of it and going north on the reach, you'll find it's all been worth while.'

Juliet gave him a withering glance which he returned with one of his tantalising grins.

'Wishing you hadn't come, little white rose?' he taunted.

'Wishing you wouldn't call me that!' she snapped.

'Think of it as a compliment. There aren't many women of your age these days who manage to retain such a look of innocence. Even Maree has more knowledge of the ways of the world than you appear to have. How come you're so trusting?'

'What makes you think I am?' she countered uneasily, aware that she had always to be on the defensive against him.

'Watching you this last week.'

Watching her! Where had he watched her? With whom had she been when he had watched her? With Gareth? No, that was impossible. When she had been with Gareth, either in his study or on the terrace, Lance had been far away inspecting the estate, sailing or fishing, or over at Glenavon visiting Alison.

'And what have you seen when you've been watching?' she countered lightly, trying to disguise the irritation she felt at the thought that he could watch her and remain unseen.

'Some things that perhaps I shouldn't have seen,' he said tantalisingly, and her eyes, sea-green and alarmed, flicked to his face. It was as usual cold-eyed, impassive, and in the brilliant clear light created by the reflection of sunlight on an expanse of water she could see lines she hadn't noticed before; lines etched by laughter at the corners of his eyes, long creases from the corners of his bold nose to the corners of his contradictory mouth, furrows ploughed across his wide forehead by thought and concentration. Everything he had done had left its mark on his face, she thought, and she felt again that strange tug at her heart which she had felt before. Perhaps she had been, and was still, guilty of condemning him unheard.

But he had said he had seen things that perhaps he shouldn't have seen. In her behaviour, perhaps? Her mind searched wildly into the recesses of her memory to discover anything she might have done during the past week to give rise to such a remark, and found nothing unusual, except the growing intimacy between Gareth and herself which had reached a climax the previous evening when he pulled her close to him, as she had wished him good night, and had kissed her on the moonlit terrace.

Again her alarmed glance flickered to Lance's face. This time his eyes met hers directly and they glinted with derision.

'I've been accused before of walking too quietly,' he observed, and she knew he had seen the incident on the terrace.

A wave of scarlet colour swept over her face as she wished suddenly and fervently that Gareth hadn't kissed her and that Lance hadn't seen.

'You seem to be making good progress in that direction,' continued Lance, still with that touch of derision.

'Well, isn't it what you wanted?' she retaliated. 'Isn't that why you invented a job for me as secretary to your mother, because you thought I might be a suitable wife for Gareth?'

It was out and lying between them, the suspicion that had been planted in her mind by a few stray remarks.

'And where, may I ask, did you get that idea?' he asked blandly.

'I've been told that you found his first wife and that you once boasted you would find him another while you were visiting London. And at Hilary's wedding you said you were there to look for a wife,' she replied as coolly as she could.

'So I did, and you took exception to my remark and attributed it to my having drunk too much champagne,' he said calmly as he began to loosen the mainsheet so that the big white mainsail eased out slowly the boat stopped plunging and its speed increased. Then he leaned forward and freed the jib sheet so that the foresail bellied out.

The sails trimmed correctly and to his satisfaction,

Lance turned and smiled at her in an indulgent, curiously avuncular fashion.

'Your notion is a romantic one, but if you like it I have no objections to it. Anything which will help Gareth recover his self-confidence is O.K. by me,' he drawled. 'Now we're on the reach, which is a much faster point of sailing. If this wind keeps up we should get to Oban by this afternoon.'

The change in the movement of the boat and the fact that she hadn't suffered a drenching recently made Juliet look about her. They had left the loch and were sailing past a rocky shore backed by wooded slopes. Looking ahead she saw a shimmering swirling stretch of water which seemed to suck the boat forward, and having seized it, swept it past a group of islands and out into a wider stretch of water across which she could see the towering bulk of a mountainous island.

Fascinated by the swift steady movement, by the glint of yellow light on the white-laced blue of the water, entranced by the brilliant greens, delicate violets and mysterious purples of the distant hills, she was silent, making no attempt to question Lance's faintly amused approval of the situation between Gareth and herself. She was still in the dark as to whether he had invented a job for her just to get her to Castle Ross to meet Gareth, but somehow out here on the sea amongst the islands it didn't matter any more, and she understood why sailing was considered such a good escape from problems associated with the land.

Eventually she was sufficiently roused from her fascinated contemplation of the seascape to ask,

'Where are we?'

'We've just come through the Sound of Luing and are now in the Firth of Lorne' replied Lance. 'That's the island of Dana over there, an isle of delight, although that description could be applied to most of the Hebridean islands.'

'It's beautiful,' she murmured. 'Could we go there?'

'Would you prefer to go there rather than go to Oban?'

he asked.

'What is there at Oban?'

'Good shops, pleasant hotels, a fishing fleet . . .'

'I think I'd prefer the island. After all, I can see shops and hotels any day in other towns, but I may not have the chance of visiting one of the islands again. It must be lovely to anchor in a sheltered bay, miles away from the mainland. It's something I've always wanted to do.'

He stared at her thoughtfully, his eyebrows raised in slight surprise. Then he glanced up at the sky. He looked at her again and smiled enigmatically and her nerves twanged suddenly with suspicion. After all, she knew so little about him and what she knew didn't endear him to her, yet here she was trusting him to take her across the sea to an isle of delight.

'If it's something you've always wanted to do then we shall do it,' he said, and his eyes glittered with excitement. 'Come hell or high water, we shall go to Dana and you shall anchor in a sheltered bay.'

It wasn't hell, but the crossing to Mull wasn't entirely comfortable and there were times when Juliet, unused to being at sea in a small boat, found it both exhilarating and frightening.

At first they made good progress even though they had to alter course and beat into the wind again. But soon the wind died away altogether and the sun shone down on the idle boat as it drifted with the tide, its sails slatting. Lance made the most of their becalmed state to leave Julie at the tiller while he went below to prepare some lunch which they ate in the cockpit.

While they were eating, cloud began to spread across the sky from the south-west and the sun lost its bright glare. Gradually the distant mountains lost their distinct violets and purples and became a uniform dull grey. A breeze sprang up, blowing out of the increasing cloud and Lance trimmed the sails accordingly so that soon the boat was running under widespread white wings of shimmering terylene directly towards the dark bulk of the isle of delight.

The wind strengthened and soon waves were building up under the hull and lifting the bow of the boat out of the water so that it seemed to surf. The effect was exciting but a little disconcerting because there were times when the boat came down off the crest of a wave and it seemed temporarily out of control, and Juliet held her breath, wondering if it was about to plunge bow first under the heaving surface of the sea, to be seen and heard of no more.

At other times when she happened to glance behind her towards the stern she gasped audibly on seeing a big wave with curling fangs higher than the boat bearing down on them and was sure that it would pour into the cockpit and swamp it completely. But always the wave collapsed just a little short of the stern and rolled under the hull.

Lance appeared not to suffer from such anxieties and controlled the movement of the tiller with little effort. He talked little, answering her questions briefly but adequately, and allayed her occasionally expressed fears with a few calm words. And gradually it occurred to her that he was an essentially uncommunicative person, quite unlike Gareth who talked incessantly about his thoughts and his feelings.

Towards the middle of the afternoon they reached a small bay where they found shelter from the swell and the wind behind a group of rocky islands. After being alone on the wide rolling sea exposed to every buffet of wave and wind, the bay was an oasis of calm pale sunlight and clear green water backed by a semi-circle of light sand-coloured cliffs.

Lance looked across at the high stone walls.

'The cliffs look interesting. I wonder if there are any caves,' he remarked. 'Shall we go ashore and explore?'

Juliet agreed eagerly, enticed by the deep green of a glen which ran inland as much as by the cliffs. The place had a romantic fairy-tale atmosphere. There was no sign if any habitation and she could readily believe that it was visited by the wee folk and the merfolk and all the other strange mythical creatures about whom Gareth had told her.

Gareth! How she wished he was there with her in the

dinghy, rowing her to the shore instead of Lance. He wouldn't sit silently. He would tell her some legend associated with the place. But Gareth couldn't have brought her here, because he was lame, paralysed by an accident while he was trying to keep up with Moira. Not for the first time Juliet found herself wondering what sort of a woman Moira had been and what had been her relationship with the man sitting opposite to her in the dinghy.

She glared at Lance, watching his averted face as he looked over his shoulder to make sure he was going the right way. Did he save all his conversation for Alison Coates whom he would marry one day if Mrs Crimond had her way?

Alison! Why wasn't she here with him? Why hadn't he invited her to come sailing with him to-day? Had they quarrelled? Or had Alison been unable to come because she had had to stay with her sick mother and he had had to find a substitute.

A substitute for Alison. That was all she was to-day? Oh, well, Alison's loss was her gain. If the lovely red-haired woman had been able to come sailing Juliet Grey would have missed not only several drenchings by spray but also the experience of coming to this island.

Still, there was something about being regarded as a mere substitute which troubled her.

'I shouldn't let it bother you,' said Lance, unexpectedly, and she jumped. He'd been watching her again and she'd forgotten to be on guard.

'Shouldn't let what bother me?' she challenged, flinging her salt-caked, wind-tumbled hair behind her shoulders.

'Being here with me,' he answered smoothly, and then grinned at her as she gasped in an exasperated manner.

'I wish you'd stop watching me, like ... like an eagle watching its prey!' she retorted.

'Why shouldn't I watch you? Your face is very pretty as well as being expressive. During the last few minutes you've looked wistful as if wishing I were someone else; then you glared at me as if you'd have liked to push me overboard; then you frowned and bit your lip, and most interesting of all, for a few seconds your eyes went quite green and you looked ready to spit and claw at the object of your jealousy. Then you looked frightened. But you often seem frightened when you're with me. Why?'

At that moment the dinghy bumped against the old stone pier. Lance shipped the oars and held on to an iron ring set in the wall of the pier. Instead of pressing her for an answer to his question he ordered her out of the dinghy.

'Be careful you don't slip on the steps,' he added. 'They're slimy through lack of use.'

Glad of the chance to get away from him for a while, Juliet mounted the steps carefully. Once at the top she didn't wait for him but ran along the derelict pier until she came to a rough road which struck off westwards, curving above a small beach of dark sand. Beyond the beach the road continued round the narrow grass-covered shore under the sheer cliffs.

She thought she heard Lance call her name, but she didn't look round to see if he was following her because a sudden impulse to annoy him, to shake his superb self-confidence, urged her onwards. The impulse was natural, the eternal feminine urge to irritate the arrogant male who thought he knew her better than she knew herself, and who considered her naïve and innocent. She had no doubt she rated as 'safe' in Lance's mind. She was someone whom he could invite to go sailing with him without having to make much effort to entertain her and without annoying his future wife. Possibly he had even told Alison last night that he had considered taking his mother's young secretary with him, and Alison had condescendingly agreed to the arrangement, knowing that there couldn't possibly be any competition.

Well, she would teach him a lesson. She would hide somewhere, and when he couldn't find her he would be worried.

She plunged on along the upper margin of a beach of boulders, sometimes following ankle-twisting tracks just above the high water mark, and sometimes scrambling across recent rock slides. Light on her feet and well-balanced, she moved quickly, flitting from rock to rock until she came to an area of flat stone just round the corner of the headland.

Above the flat plateau there was a wide opening in the cliff. Juliet entered the opening and found herself in a huge cave. Near the entrance there was a large boulder. She ducked behind it, and completely hidden from the view of anyone looking into the cave she sat down.

As her eyes gradually grew accustomed to the dim light she could see carved into the rough stone of the wall above her crosses and other symbols, sure signs that the cave had once been used as shelter by man. The wall on the other side was damper and was covered with moss, and from the roof of the cave on that side near the entrance water dripped in a steady stream.

Turning her back to the boulder and hugging her knees to her chin, Juliet decided she would stay there until Lance arrived. She was sure he would come and that he would call her name. She wouldn't answer straight away, just to tantalise him. She had never tantalised anyone in this way before and it gave her a curious sense of power plus excitement. He would be anxious in case she had an accident, because accidents happened to people when they were with him.

Her thoughts pulled up short. Where had she got that idea? From the curious conversation which had taken place the day Lance had arrived at Castle Ross when Gareth had refused to let Maree go fishing with Lance and the girl had accused her father of not letting her go with her uncle because her mother had been with Lance when she had been killed. Where and how had Moira been killed, and why had she been with Lance?

Too many questions and too few answers, thought Juliet disgustedly. She ought to ask Lance himself. But he would only tell her in that icy way of his not to concern herself with anything beyond her work.

She realised suddenly that she had been sitting behind the boulder for some time and he hadn't come. No voice had called her name. Supposing he hadn't seen her enter the cave? Supposing he had gone straight past along the shore?

The cave was echoing with the sound of the sea smashing against the rocks. It seemed much noisier than when she had entered. The tide must be coming in and covering the plateau of rock outside. It was time for her to move if only to ensure that she could get back along the shore to the pier.

Feeling slightly disappointed because she had not been able to tantalise Lance, she went to the entrance of the cave. She was greeted by a sight which sent icy prickles of panic chasing up and down her spine. The flat area of stone was covered by greenish-grey swirling water and as she gaped a wave reared up and crashed over the edge of the plateau and greedy fingers of water spread right into the cave. It was followed almost at once by another wave, and looking beyond the spray and spume, she saw the whole sea was a heaving mass of white-topped waves being pushed against the land by the wind which had increased in strength and which was now moaning eerily in the hollows of the cliffs.

Gingerly she inched forward and peered round the edge of the cave entrance. The path she had followed under the towering wall of cliffs had disappeared under tossing water which flung itself against the foot of the headland. She was cut off, imprisoned by angry hissing water which looked as if it might invade the cave.

> ⁸ "Break, break, break,
>   On thy cold gray stones, O Sea." '

The voice spoke behind her. For another wild moment of panic she thought she was imagining it, then a hand touched her shoulder and she knew with a strange quiver of relief that Lance was really there in the cave with her. But how had he got there without her seeing him? Anger that he had walked in silently and unseen shook her, and with a wriggle of her shoulders she broke free of his hold and whirled round to face him.

> ' "And I would that my tongue could utter
> The thoughts that arise in me," '

she spat out furiously.

He laughed appreciatively.

'You're much quicker on the draw than one would expect from looking at you,' he remarked. 'I've often wondered how that verse ended. But I don't suppose Tennyson's thoughts were at all like yours are at present. I guess you're angry with me.'

'Yes, I am. How dare you creep up behind me like that and frighten me!' she fumed. 'How did you get in here without me seeing you or hearing you?'

'I walked in the same way that you did. I walk quietly— remember?'

'Then why didn't you call my name and tell me you were here?'

He stood, hands in his trouser pockets, considering her thoughtfully, that faint enigmatic smile curving his mouth.

'Well now, that's hard to explain,' he drawled. 'I had the impression that you were deliberately hiding from me when I came into the cave, and I remembered how irritated I used to get when I was a boy if I'd found a good hiding place and I was found too soon. So I thought I'd let you enjoy your hiding place and let you stay hidden for a while. Also I thought it would teach you a lesson for running off the way you did.'

Teach her a lesson! Her own words concerning him. Juliet gritted her teeth. He was making fun of her, treating her like a child with whom he'd condescended to play a game of hide and seek. He hadn't been worried about her one little bit.

'How long have you been here?' she asked.

95

'A few minutes less than you. And now it's my turn to ask a question. Why did you run away and hide?'

Still furious at the treatment handed out to her by him, she had no answer ready because she no longer understood her own impulse to annoy him—an impulse which had landed them both in their present predicament.

'I ... I don't know,' she muttered, just as water ugly and edged with white foam swirled about her feet. 'Oh, what shall we do? The water is going to flood the cave. Where shall we go?' she exclaimed.

He took her arm and pulled her back into the darker recesses of the cave.

'It won't come any farther than the entrance,' he said calmly.

'How do you know?' she asked.

'There's a line of seaweed where the high water stops. Beyond that the floor of the cave if fairly dry.'

'How long do you think we'll be here?'

'About an hour ... maybe a little longer. It depends on the weather. It's deteriorating and the wind tends to keep the tide pushed in for longer than normal.'

'But there was no sign of a storm when we left the boat.'

'Yes, there was. There've been signs of storm all afternoon in the sky. I've been watching it grow.'

'You didn't say anything,' she accused.

'I'd no idea then that you were going to go exploring on your own as soon as we came ashore,' he remarked dryly. 'I called after you to suggest you didn't go far because the tide was coming in. But you weren't listening.'

'And now we're both stuck here until the tide goes out, and it's my fault,' she moaned. 'Oh, you must think I'm very foolish.'

'And trusting.'

'Wet behind the ears, you said the other day.'

'Did I? Not very polite of me, but truthful. More truthful than your answer to my question a few minutes ago. Why did you run away, Juliet?'

In the half-light of the cave he seemed big and over-powering. She guessed he was capable of forcing an answer out of her, but the spark of rebelliousness which had made her run away from him was still alight. Flinging back her head, her face and hair pale blurs in the dimness, she looked up at him and retorted,

'Perhaps because I'm not so trusting after all. I don't trust you.'

'You expect me to believe that?' he said scornfully. 'Since you don't trust me why did you come sailing to-day? Come on, now let's have the truth. Why did you run away?'

'I wanted to teach you a lesson,' she muttered.

'That makes two of us. But why should you want to teach me a lesson? What have I done?'

'You take me for granted. You're so smug, especially back there in the dinghy, making out that you know me better than I know myself, so I thought I'd hide somewhere and then when you couldn't find me you'd be worried in case something had happened to me!' she burst out, then as she realised he was beginning to laugh at her, her temper seethed and she went the whole way and added, 'You wouldn't want an accident to happen to me while I'm with you, would you?'

That stopped his laughter and she saw his shoulders stiffen. But when he answered her he was still coolly in command of himself.

'Naturally I wouldn't want you to have an accident whether you're with me or whether you're not. I'm not the sort of person who goes around wishing accidents on others out of petty spite.'

'But people tend to have accidents when they're in your company, don't they, because you like to take risks. You like living with the edge of danger and you're contemptuous of those who can't or who won't . . . like Gareth.'

The silence which followed her words was so fraught with tension that she began to wish she hadn't spoken so boldly.

'I suppose I have him to thank for this load of drivel,' he

remarked rather wearily at last. 'What has he told you about accidents happening to people who go with me?'

'Nothing really,' she admitted reluctantly. 'But Maree said that her mother was with you when she was killed and I heard Gareth say to Mrs Crimond that if he hadn't let Moira go with you she might be alive now.'

She waited hopefully for his reply, because now was his chance to tell her how Moira had died and possibly clear up the doubts in her mind about his relationship with his sister-in-law.

'And consequently your curiosity was aroused,' he murmured. Then with a quick change of manner, his voice icy, he added, 'I thought I'd told you that anything beyond your work at Castle Ross was not your concern.'

'Yes, you did, but I couldn't help hearing what was said,' she whispered, backing away from him.

'And now you know that Gareth blames me for Moira's death,' he said, following her slowly, looming over her, a threatening shadow. 'And you've believed him, haven't you?'

She couldn't answer because her throat had dried up. She tried to back away from him again, but he was too quick. He tucked two fingers inside the turtle neck of her sweater and pulled her gently towards him.

'Haven't you, Juliet?' he persisted.

'Yes,' she admitted.

'Then you'll realise that because he believes what he does about me and because he feels the way he does about you he's going to go through hell to-night wondering where you and I are and what we're doing together.'

'I ... I don't understand. I thought we were going back to the castle.'

'There's no way we can reach Castle Ross before to-morrow. To-night you and I shall sleep aboard the boat, that is if we ever get back to it.'

CHAPTER FOUR

LANCE'S voice was a low murmur and his breath fanned her cheek as he bent his head close to hers. Juliet closed her eyes. She hoped that when she opened them she would find herself back in bed at Castle Ross, and all that had happened since she had woken that morning would recede into the depths of her subconscious; a dream, nothing more.

But when she opened her eyes she was still there in the sea-echoing, dimly-lit vault and Lance's fingers were still in the collar of her sweater, warm and rough against the skin of her throat, sending an uncontrollable tingling sensation through her body. She was so close to him that she could see the glint in his eyes as he looked down at her.

'We must get back to-day,' she insisted rather wildly. 'What will they think when we don't return?'

He released her sweater and plunged his hands into his pockets again.

'You should have thought of that earlier,' he said coldly. 'You realised surely that you threw away any possibility of us returning to Castle Ross to-day when you asked if we could come to Dana when there was a storm in the offing. If we'd gone to Oban instead you'd have been able to leave the boat and return to Lochmoyhead by bus. A phone call from there would have brought McVinn out to pick you up in the estate car. As it is, the situation in which you now find yourself is really of your own making.'

Juliet couldn't remember having felt so angry in her life. It seemed to her that he was actually blaming her for the predicament in which they now found themselves.

'How was I to know that?' she exclaimed. 'Oh, you're no better than Maree! You take advantage too. You've taken advantage of my ignorance about sailing, about distances and about storms. You could have refused to bring me here.'

99

As usual he didn't retaliate to her furiously flung words but took time to consider what she had said, his head bent as he kicked idly at the stony debris on the floor of the cave, and his calmness made her even more cross.

'True,' he admitted at last, 'I could have refused, and what would you have thought of me then? I brought you here against my better judgement in order to grant your wish to see one of the islands while you had the opportunity. Seems to me you're very hard to please, Juliet.'

While she was still gasping he moved away from her into the back of the cave, leaving her to ponder his words. He had granted her wish because it had been in his power to do so and for that she should be grateful instead of accusing him of taking advantage of her. The now familiar tug at her heart made her aware that once again she had been guilty of misjudging him. This time the urge to apologise to him was strong.

But he was nowhere to be seen.

'Lance!' she called tentatively, moving towards the dark wall of rock at the back of the cave.

'Over here,' he answered. 'I've found somewhere to sit. Sandstone is very obliging—it provides ledges for sitting on, this one is rather narrow, but it serves. I must bring Jamie here some day. He'd be interested in the rock formation.'

His cool matter-of-fact voice relieved her, but also made her hesitant about offering an apology. He must have decided to dismiss their recent confrontation and she decided against reviving it. She stood uncertainly before him, and he put out a hand, gripped her arm and pulled her forward,

'Come and sit down,' he ordered.

She obeyed. There wasn't much room and her shoulder and knee brushed against him as she balanced rather precariously on the stone seat. He put an arm round her waist to keep her from falling off. The warmth and strength of his body struck through her, sending alarm signals in all directions. She stiffened involuntarily, but his arm didn't relax.

'There's scarcely room for two,' he murmured, 'but like this we'll be fairly comfortable for the next half-hour or so.'

Little shudders ran through her body. Hoping to divert his attention from her shaking, she burst into speech.

'Do you know any stories about the cave or about this part of the island?' she quavered, and her voice sounded unnaturally high.

'All I can tell you is that the area of sandstone in front of the cave is what is known as a tidal quarry and has probably been used for centuries and even quite recently. Slabs of stone can be detached by driving wooden wedges into the horizontal cracks. Sea water does the rest of the work by forcing the stone apart.

'Where would it be used?' she asked, interested and forgetting her fear of him.

'For ornamental carvings in Iona Cathedral, which isn't very far from here, and also in the doors and window facings of old chapels on the island. Some of the carving must have been done by the monks and the craftsmen years ago in this cave. Did you notice the symbols carved into the wall?'

'Yes, I found several crosses and something which looked like a windmill and some leaf designs rather like a shamrock.'

'They're probably the trademarks of individual workmen. I found a carving of a rose, so I think I'll give the cave a new name.'

'What is its name?'

'I believe it's called Uamh nan Cailleach, which is Gaelic for the Cave of the Old Woman, but I'm going to call it the Cave of the White Rose, because I found myself having to put in an hour or two with you here.'

She knew he was teasing her, but his mention of the white rose made her aware of him again and she tried to move away from him, but couldn't.

'Don't move so violently,' he warned. 'You'll fall off. I'm sorry my story-telling isn't up to Gareth's standard. My

101

abilities tend to be on the practical side.'

'A man of action,' murmured Juliet, in retaliation for the white rose. 'Your mother told me that you preferred actions to words and that often made you seem ruthless, and inconsiderate of the feelings of others.'

Almost at once she wished she had kept her mouth shut, because his arm tightened round her waist ominously.

'So that's why you're afraid of me,' he mocked.

'I'm not afraid,' she denied weakly.

'Then why have you avoided me all week? And why are you shaking now? Is it possible that you're afraid of the next action I might take?'

There was a dangerous edge to his voice. The palm of his hand slid against her cheek as he forced her face round. She closed her eyes and willed herself to ignore the fire which scorched through her veins at the touch of his hand on her skin.

'Now, what happens next?' he said, and once more laughter threaded its way through his voice. 'Useless for you to scream here, because there isn't anyone to hear you. You could slap my face, I suppose.'

Outraged and bewildered by his easy mockery, Juliet tried to free herself. Then, unable to break that steel-like grip, she searched for words to fling at him.

'You ... you ... you're...' she spluttered, and then words failed too.

'I know,' he replied accommodatingly. 'I'm unkind, inconsiderate, shameless. But no more shameless than you are for believing that I break rules.'

'Gareth says you make your own rules,' she flung at him, stung into replying because he had guessed so accurately why she was afraid of him.

'Perhaps I have in some cases, but I've never broken any where innocents like you are concerned, and I'm not going to start now.'

He released her suddenly and slid off the ledge, and walked away. Unable to keep her precarious position on the ledge without his support, Juliet slid off too.

'Where are you going?' she enquired timidly, as her anger dissipated.

'To see if the tide has started to go out,' he said carelessly over his shoulder and she felt suddenly cold as his interest was removed from her. Not wanting to be left alone she followed him to the entrance of the cave.

The force of the wind sent her hair streaming back from her face and flung stinging, salty spray into her face. Flying spindrift had reduced visibility to a greenish-grey blur in which it was impossible to distinguish sky from sea. Waves were still pounding on the sandstone plateau, but the insidious spreading fingers of water no longer reached as far as the new line of damp dark seaweed which curved at her feet.

'It's on the turn,' observed Lance, 'but it will be some time before we'll be able to make our way along the shore. You can see now why it's impossible for us to sail back to Castle Ross to-day. The risk would be too great.'

'But I thought you liked taking risks.'

He turned a narrowed grey glance on her.

'Seems to me you've thought a lot about me,' he jibed, and in spite of the cool spray, her face felt hot. 'Yes, sometimes I do take risks, just as I'm capable of making my own rules. But ever since I made its acquaintance as a boy I've had a great respect for the sea. When it's in this mood it's safer to stay on the shore.'

As she stood there beside him watching the monotonous advance and retreat of the waves, feeling completely isolated from the rest of the world, it occurred to Juliet that he had been in a similar situation before when he had been snowbound in the Cairngorms with Moira, and Gareth had gone through hell wondering where they were and what they were doing. Had he been granting Moira's wish by taking her skiing when a blizzard was imminent?

Her thoughts rankled and she turned back into the cave in an attempt to change their direction. Going over to the west wall, she stared at the carved symbols. With one finger she traced the outline of a simple cross, then a shamrock, then a letter 'W' and on until she came to the unmistakable carving of the flower of a wild rose, and suddenly she was standing again in the busy entrance hall of a London hotel and Lance was tucking a long-stemmed white rosebud behind her ear and saying *You might call it symbolic*. Now she knew he had meant the rosebud had been symbolic of her innocence—and he had just told her that he didn't break rules concerning innocents like her.

The outline of the rose blurred a little and her finger shook. In spite of what he had said she was still afraid of him, but not because of any action he might take. She wasn't afraid of what he might do but of her own reactions to him; afraid of the effect he had on her emotions.

She glanced over her shoulder fearfully, remembering his strange ability to guess at her thoughts. He was still leaning against the wall of the cave just inside the entrance watching the sea, so still and absorbed he could have been in a trance. But as she looked he moved and stepped out of the cave. In a few seconds he was back and calling to her,

'Come and look outside.'

She went, following him out on to the wet stone and looking where he pointed to the cliffs down which waterfalls were descending only to be checked by the strong wind which blew them back like smoke to the rim of the cliffs high above.

'I've heard that that could happen, but I've never seen it before,' said Lance, excitement crisping his voice.

'"A land of streams! some, like a downward smoke, Slow-dropping veils of thinnest lawn, did go,"' murmured Juliet, staring fascinated at the white mist.

He turned to her with a quizzical lift of his eyebrows.

'More poetry?' he queried

'Tennyson again,' she replied.

He eyed her narrowly again, and then his mouth twisted cynically.

'No wonder you and Gareth deal well together. You must enjoy quoting poetry to each other,' he jibed, and turning away he pointed to the path which was just appearing, a series of puddles winding under the cliff. 'It won't be long now before we can leave this place.'

He sounded as if he would be glad to leave it, and the jibe about her and Gareth hurt, reminding her that he was unkind and unpredictable. She wanted to tell him that she didn't quote poetry to Gareth for the simple reason that Gareth talked so much when she was with him that she didn't get a chance. She wanted to tell him that only here with him, encouraged by his own deep-voiced utterance earlier and now by his obvious delight at the sight of the windblown cascades of water, had she felt the need to quote poetry in an attempt to reach out to him and to show she shared his delight.

'Are you hungry?' he asked suddenly, and she blinked, more than a little bewildered by her surprising thoughts.

'Yes, I suppose I am.'

'Then I think it's time we made a move. The going will be rather soggy underfoot, but if you keep close behind me and follow in my footsteps you should be all right.' He sounded impatient now, and she guessed that he had had enough of being alone with her in a cave. A man of action, he disliked being inactive. 'Supper will be out of cans,' he added, 'but I can safely promise you fresh trout for breakfast.'

The walk back was wet and uncomfortable and by the time they reached the pier they were both wet and chilly, a state which wasn't improved during the journey back to the yacht in the dinghy.

Once aboard Lance ordered her to go below and came down himself after checking the anchor. He showed Juliet where the canned goods were stored and then busied himself lighting the Primus cooker. The meal wasn't exciting, but it was filling, and the heat from the cooker and from the Tilley lamp which Lance had lit soon thawed out the chill in Juliet's bones.

After they had eaten she washed up the dishes while Lance went once more to inspect the anchor. He came back to inform her that he had decided to put out a storm anchor to ensure that the boat wouldn't drag out of position during the night. From the shelter of the cabin she watched through a porthole as he rowed out in the dinghy, a big fisherman anchor propped up in its stern which was attached by a stout line to the bow of the boat. When he had rowed far enough away from the boat he stopped and standing up in the dinghy heaved the anchor overboard, then came back.

Satisfied that the boat was safe for the night, he joined her in the cabin again and producing a pack of cards suggested that they played gin rummy. It was warm and quiet in the cabin and the gentle swinging movement of the boat had a soporific effect on Juliet so that she had difficulty in keeping her eyes open long enough to concentrate on her cards.

'Are you sleepy?' asked Lance.

She looked up and nodded.

'Then go to bed,' he said gently.

Bewildered, she looked round the cabin, wondering how and where she was to go to bed.

'Here's a sleeping bag and a pillow,' he said, producing them out of a locker behind him. 'If you'd like to go and wash up for'ard I'll get your bed ready for you.'

In the forecastle she did her best with her tangle of hair, and rinsed and dried her face which glowed after its exposure to the elements. When she returned to the cabin Lance had gone and she could hear him moving about on deck. On the berth on which she had been sitting the sleeping bag had been arranged and unzipped and the pillow placed at one end. Juliet slumped down for a moment on the berth. The long day in the open air plus the strain of being on the defensive with Lance had taken their toll. She longed for bed, but wondered when once she was in the sleeping bag curled up on the bunk whether she would sleep knowing that he would be there lying on the opposite bunk!

Slowly she removed her sweater and shoes, climbed into the bag and zipped it up. For a few seconds she lay blinking drowsily at the flaring lamp and listening to the creak of the boat as it swung in the gusts of wind which shook it. Her eyes closed involuntarily and she slept at once.

They breakfasted on fresh trout as Lance had promised. He had caught them from the burn which hid amongst the tall trees in the green glen. He had caught them by hand by a method he called 'guddling'. Juliet wished she had been with him to see him do it, but he had gone ashore early, long before she had wakened.

She ate every morsel of her succulent fish and even enjoyed the tea without milk. She had a wonderful sense of well-being, which surprised her. It was all to do with having slept soundly and having woken to the sight of golden light shimmering on the ceiling of the cabin and the smell of the trout being cooked.

After opening her eyes she had lain still for a while and had watched Lance as he had bent over his cooking, his jaw blurred with dark stubble, his hair slipping forward on his forehead, and she had thought how pleasant it was to know that someone capable was in charge of everything; that for once she didn't have to do the planning and be on the alert for all eventualities. And a new and startling thought had leapt through her mind. How lovely it would be if it could always be like that!

Then Lance had turned his head. His cold clear eyes had looked at her, through her and had dismissed her, and she'd known a strange sense of loss because he didn't share her thought.

When breakfast was over they made preparations for departure. Lance went out in the dinghy and hauled up the big anchor, brought it aboard and stowed it away. Then he hoisted the mainsail. It flapped idly because there was little wind in the bay behind the islands. Telling Juliet to keep the boat pointed in the direction from which the wind was blowing, he went forward and pulled up the other anchor, then returned to the cockpit to take the tiller from her. The mainsail filled with the slight wind and the boat moved out of the anchorage.

As she looked back at the green glen and the towering cliffs Juliet knew she would never forget Dana. As they cleared the entrance to the bay she could see the opening of the cave above the plateau of sandstone. The Cave of the White Rose. It was there that she had clashed with the enigmatic man who had brought her sailing. It seemed to her that she understood him less than before because, although she had been so close to him both physically and mentally for a short time, she found now that he had withdrawn behind a film of ice which she had no way of cracking.

The sail back to Loch Moy, although not as exciting as that of the previous day, provided its own colour and breathtaking views. It was a day of alternating cloud and sunshine with a steady wind which made it possible for them to reach Castle Ross in the early afternoon.

Leaving the boat at its mooring, they walked up the path from the shore and approached the terrace. A tall figure limped out of the lounge, and Lance broke his long silence.

'Your gentle knight awaits you,' he mocked. 'Didn't I say he'd be anxious? Anxiety has actually brought him to his feet!' He sounded pleased, almost complacently so, and Juliet glanced at him in surprise. He was watching Gareth and the cold assessing light in his eyes caused a return of all the dislike she had ever felt for him.

'Juliet, are you all right?' Gareth's voice was harsh with anxiety. He was hobbling down the steps and he was without his stick. She had never thought she would see him move so quickly. Above him on the terrace there was a movement. A bright green dress topped by red hair glowed against the mellow stone of the castle as Alison moved forward to wait and watch by the steps.

Gareth took hold of Juliet's hands. His blue gaze roved over her and then flashed to Lance.

'What happened? Where have you been?' he rapped autocratically and for a brief moment there was a faint resemblance between him and his eldest brother.

'You know,' returned Lance easily, almost insolently. 'I

108

took Juliet sailing.'

'That wasn't all. Why didn't you come back last night?'

'We went to Dana Island.'

'In that storm?' Gareth's voice expressed disbelief.

'We arrived before the storm broke. There was no way we could come back until it had blown out, and by then we had our heads down and were fast asleep.'

A dull red stained Gareth's thin face and an ugly glint appeared in his eyes. His hands tightened painfully on Juliet's.

'That sounds a familiar story. It's time you thought up another, Lance,' he remarked.

Lance chose to ignore the sneer as Alison came down the steps.

'Hello, Alison,' he said, and a warm smile lit his eyes. 'Have you been offering comfort to the anxious?'

'No, she hasn't,' interjected Gareth. 'All she does is nag, nag, nag about my leg. She hasn't given me a minute's peace all week-end. As if I didn't have enough of her yesterday when we went visiting to Glenavon she has to come over this afternoon. Why don't you go home now, Alison? Lance is here at last, and I'm sure he'll be only too pleased to drive you.'

Alison's topaz-coloured eyes were puzzled as she glanced at him.

'I shall go in a few minutes,' she said coolly. 'But Lance doesn't have to take me because he's going to be busy. Your mother has just received a phone call from Elstone. There's been an accident.'

'Jamie,' said Lance quietly.

Alison turned to look at him her eyes widening slightly. 'How did you know?' she asked.

His big shoulders lifted and dropped.

'I don't know. I've had the feeling all morning that I shouldn't have gone sailing, that I should have gone up there yesterday. Is he trapped?'

'Yes. Your mother has all the details. The leader of the expedition rang up. He wanted to speak to you. I think

109

you'd better go and see her Lance. She wants to go up there.'

He didn't wait to listen to any more but sprang up the steps and disappeared into the house.

Alison turned to looked at Juliet. Her glance took in the tangled pale hair, wind-burnt face and creased clothing and a faint, slightly patronising smile curved her mouth.

'I expect you're feeling in need of a bath and a change,' she said. 'Lance should never have taken you so far.'

'No, he shouldn't,' put in Gareth. 'A sail down the loch and back would have been enough. But then he has never considered anyone else's feelings. I suppose he decided on the spur of the moment that he wanted to and you had to go too whether you wanted to or not.'

'I asked him to take me to Dana,' said Juliet quietly, feeling the time had come for her to take the responsibility for the previous day's events.

'You asked him? Why?' exclaimed Gareth.

'It seemed to be an interesting place to go, and it was. We found a cave in the cliffs and saw the wind blowing the water back up the cliffs just as it's described in *The Lotus-Eaters*,' she replied, wanting to share with him the pleasure she had known, sure he would understand at once. But the blue eyes held no warmth for once as they met hers.

'I don't understand why on earth anyone would want to go all that way on an afternoon like yesterday afternoon just to see a cave,' he replied.

'Well, evidently Juliet thought it was worthwhile being knocked about on the boat and having to sleep in her clothing,' murmured Alison. 'I can't say I'd enjoy such an outing. And it isn't done, you know, my dear,' she said with a touch of condescension, 'to stay away all night with one's employer. The family might understand, but just imagine what Vinnie and the other people on the estate must be saying and thinking about you! Everyone knows you went with Lance because Mrs Crimond was so upset when you didn't return that she wanted a search party organised.'

Whatever had given her the idea that Alison was a warm,

110

kind-hearted person? thought Juliet miserably. Spite had flickered out of every word the woman had just spoken.

'But she must have known I'd be all right with Lance. You must have known that,' she said appealingly to Gareth.

'I know no such thing,' he returned coldly. He tried to move forward and then winced. 'Damn, I forgot my stick.'

'I'll go and get it,' said Alison, and swept gracefully up the steps.

'Don't bother. Juliet will help me,' said Gareth. His hand came down on Juliet's shoulder, reassuring her, comforting her in the face of Alison's spite, and she smiled up at him gratefully.

As they mounted the steps slowly Alison watched them.

'A very touching sight,' she remarked with a touch of sarcasm. 'But you know, Gareth, you went down those steps as if nothing was wrong with your leg apart from a little stiffness due to misuse. Regular exercising would cure that. I think Lance is right when he says your lameness is purely psychosomatic. You're only lame because you've been made to think you're lame. You've worried yourself into being lame.'

'Go home, Alison!' he answered through clenched teeth. 'I've had enough of your advice.'

'All right, I'm going. Don't let him lean on you too heavily, Juliet,' she added. 'I know you mean well, but Gareth is much stronger than you in many ways and he'd soon wear you out.'

With a swirl of her green skirt and a toss of her red hair she went into the house, while under his breath Gareth called her a rude name.

'Take no notice of her, Juliet. She loves to think she can boss everyone around. She and Lance are well suited.' He lowered himself on to the chaise-longue and looked up at her. 'I hope he treated you well.'

'Yes, he did. He granted my wish. Now please excuse me. I must go and change my clothes and go to see Mrs Crimond. She must be very worried.'

'She was distracted last night wondering what she would

do if Lance were drowned, and I ... well, I don't mind admitting I went through hell too. Juliet, you must know...'

'Juliet,' the crisp voice spoke from the French window. Lance was there, still in his sailing clothes, his face still unshaven, its expression grim. 'My mother would like to see you.'

It was an order and she obeyed, flitting past him without looking at either him or Gareth, concerned only with what Mrs Crimond might say to her. Would she reprimand her for going with Lance? Would she say what Alison had said, that it wasn't done to stay out all night with one's employer?

But as soon as she walked into the study she knew that Mrs Crimond was thinking nothing of the sort, because the novelist greeted her with outstretched arms and held her closely for a moment.

'I'm so glad to see you safe and sound. It was naughty of Lance to take you away like that, and I've told him so.'

'I asked him to take me to Dana,' said Juliet quickly.

'But even so he should have known better than to take you so far. I don't know what he was thinking of. Thank heaven he's come back in time. Have you heard about Jamie? There's my poor baby trapped in an underground cave now.'

'Yes, Miss Coates mentioned it.'

'Dear Alison! Such a tower of strength in time of need. What a comfort she's been. But now you're back and I want you to come with me and Lance to Elstone this afternoon. It will help me to have you there while waiting for news. Lance will, I expect, want to go and help with the rescue. So as soon as you can change and pack a few clothes we'll set off. Oh, to think of poor Jamie trapped underground! Why will these boys have such dangerous hobbies? Why do they never learn what anxieties they cause me?'

On the way to her room Juliet met Lance coming up the stairs again. He followed her to the top landing where she turned to speak to him.

'Is it really necessary for Mrs Crimond to go to Elstone?' she asked.

The curl to his mouth wasn't pleasant.

'You don't want to go. You'd prefer to stay with Gareth and hold hands,' he accused.

'No, no, it isn't that. I just wondered what use she could possibly be up there. Won't it task her nerves even more than they're tasked already?'

'She wants to go, and I think that provided she has you there for company she'll be better there close to Jamie than sitting here and fretting. For one thing she'll understand better what's happening, and for another her being there will help Jamie.'

'Are they in contact with him?' she asked.

'Yes. I've just talked to Graham Lee, the leader of the expedition. They know where he is and they can hear him when he speaks to them. He says he's broken an arm. There's a girl trapped with him.' He pushed the hair back off his forehead with an impatient gesture. 'You take the bathroom first, and hurry,' he ordered tersely.

Suddenly it was important that he shouldn't think badly of her, that he should know she didn't want to stay with Gareth and hold his hand, that she wanted to help if she could.

'If you really think it will help your mother if I go with her I'll be glad to go,' she said urgently. 'And I'm sure it will help Jamie a great deal to know that *you* are going to help rescue him.'

He swung round, surprise and puzzlement breaking up the usual impassivity of his face. Then he grinned.

'Why, Juliet, could it be that you're beginning to appreciate my worth after all?' he mocked softly, and her face went pink. With a quick change of tone he snapped, 'Now, hurry,' and went into his room.

On the journey north Julie sat in the front of the car next to Lance. He said that he hoped to reach Inverpool, a fishing port on the north-west coast, by seven o'clock that evening.

113

As the crow flew the distance was only ninety-five miles, but looking at the route they would have to follow in order to avoid impassable mountains and which took them first to Oban, then to Ballachulish Ferry and on through the Great Glen right across to the east coast of the country before they could start approaching the port, Juliet thought he was over-optimistic. However, they made fairly good progress on an afternoon in which sunshine and cloud alternately highlighted and dimmed the landscape.

Gradually the Highlands unfolded before her fascinated eyes. In turn she admired the lovely Loch Linnhe, a blue slash of water between emerald and bottle green shores, noted the simple white-washed elegance of small towns and villages, looked with awe at mysterious majestic mountains, some grey and forbidding in the shadow of clouds, others purple and warmly enticing in the sunlight. When they approached the east coast the flatter, more arable land came as a surprise before they turned north-west into a forest of mountains and deep glens.

As usual Lance had little to say except to make an occasional derogatory remark about the narrowness of the roads. At one point he said to his mother that he should have invested in a small light aeroplane instead of a sailing boat.

'But I couldn't have come with you in a plane,' objected Mrs Crimond. 'No, Lance, a car is quite fast and dangerous enough.'

'Not in an emergency like this when you want to travel directly and not on an everlasting switchback,' he growled, as he pulled the car round yet another hairpin bend.

'Your trouble is that you got too used to fast travel when you were in Canada. Think of all the beauty we would have missed this afternoon if we'd come by plane. Aren't you glad you came, Juliet, or do you find the journey as frustrating as Lance does?'

'Oh, no. I think the glens and the mountains are beautiful. I'd no idea that there was so much natural wild scenery in Britain,' replied Juliet.

'Then you might spare a thought for the conservancy people who are making sure it's kept natural and wild—and remember that a few good roads wouldn't spoil it in any way,' said Lance.

They reached Inverpool just before half past six. A rainbow curved over the white houses, its spectrum of colours brilliant against the blue-black of sky and mountain. From there it was only a few miles to Elstone, the small town where some of the cavers were staying, and they passed through more wild romantic country dominated by the evening silhouettes of two towering mountains against a sky which had changed to lemon colour. But as they dropped down a hill into the town Lance pointed out a change in the landscape in the distance. In the evening light the sharply-edged outcrops of some hills were milky white, and at once Juliet recognised a similarity to the hills surrounding the Cauldron, near Castle Ross. They had come at last to the country of the underground caves.

They went straight to the small gabled country hotel where some of the cavers were staying and where two rooms had been reserved for them. The leader of the expedition, a tall man called Graham Lee, was there to greet them and to assure Mrs Crimond that Jamie was alive and cheerful.

'But I'm glad you came, Lance, because I'm thinking we'll have to blast the rock to get to him and I'll be glad of your help. Morley is up there now and laying the charges, Jamie'll be glad to hear your voice, I'm thinking, so if you wouldn't mind coming up to the site now . . .?'

'Yes, I'll come straight away,' replied Lance readily.

'Lance, you'll be careful, please,' pleaded his mother, but her plea fell on deaf ears, for he was already walking away with Graham.

Mrs Crimond's glance was rueful as she looked round the homely hotel lounge.

'You see what I mean, Juliet,' she sighed. 'We've hardly arrived and he has to go rushing off to the caves, leaving us to take care of ourselves. And it isn't just the thought of Jamie which is taking him there but the prospect of the danger involved in rescuing him. He could have seen us settled in before going up there.'

'I don't think so,' replied Juliet, who found it difficult to imagine Lance overseeing the settling in of two women into a hotel while other people tried to rescue his brother. 'You wanted him to be like that, you know, a lion in battle. You wanted all your sons to be adventurous or you wouldn't have called them after King Arthur's knights.'

'Yes, I know. But remember that the knights were also gallant and gentle when in the society of women. Those characteristics seem to be totally lacking in Lance, whereas Gareth has them to excess and isn't at all adventurous.'

'Not physically, perhaps,' argued Juliet gently, rather surprised at herself, 'but his mind goes adventuring into the world of philosophy.'

Mrs Crimond stared at her with her brow creased in thought. Then she leaned forward and patted Juliet's hand.

'I'm so glad you understand Gareth. I used to feel that Moira didn't. She was so active, not in the least romantic, and I've often wondered if they were really happy together during the last few years.'

The last few years when Lance had been back from Canada; when he'd taken Moira skiing and sailing, granting her wishes because it had been in his power to do so while his brother had been helpless. Why had he granted her wishes? Because he had loved her, had always loved her and should have married her, perhaps? Had that been the situation? And was it the reason for the antagonism between Gareth and Lance now? Had Lance lost Moira to Gareth originally because he lacked gallantry and gentleness?

So wondered Juliet, trying as always to solve the enigma of her employer. Since last night she was finding it difficult to continue to dislike him. Although she agreed with Mrs Crimond that he didn't show the obvious social graces like Gareth did, he had shown gallantry and gentleness to her in other ways. He had used his skill as a sailor of small boats to take her to an island of delight. He had calmed her fears

116

when they had been cut off by the tide in the cave. He had seen that she was warm and comfortable before she slept. He had caught and cooked fresh fish for her breakfast. Oh, yes, there were many ways in which a man could show gallantry to a woman, and they weren't always obvious.

There wasn't much spare room in the hotel, the proprietress explained as she took them upstairs, and she hoped they wouldn't mind sharing a room. She had put up a temporary bed in Jamie's room for Lance. She was sure they must be hungry after their long drive and when they had washed and freshened themselves a little they would find a wee bite of supper in the dining-room.

The 'wee bite' consisted of a mixed grill, home-baked scones and jam, and an enormous pot of tea. While they were eating, Mrs Robertson, the proprietress, brought in a young man who had just come down from the caves and who was able to give them a first-hand account of how Jamie had been trapped while he sat down to eat with them. His name was Eric Woodsworth and he explained that he was also a sub-aqua diver.

'But why is it necessary for you to have diving experience?' asked Juliet.

'Well, at the moment we're only investigating the entrances to the system of caves, and since there's a considerable flow of water in the passages a lot of exploring has to be done underwater.'

'Have you had any success this time?'

'We were doing fine. Laura—that's Laura Penny who is trapped with Jamie just now—managed to wriggle into a crack in the rock which we knew must lead to a bigger cave. She reported that there were no further large openings, so we decided to blast. That's what we've been doing most of the week.'

'Surely blasting is dangerous,' said Mrs Crimond. 'No wonder there was a rock fall.'

'It is dangerous, and very small quantities of explosive are used, just enough to enlarge a crack to remove obstruction so that a good caver can worm his way through.'

117

'So I gather you made a way and that good caver who wormed his way through was Jamie,' said Mrs Crimond with a touch of dryness.

'That's it,' said Eric with a sheepish grin. 'Jamie went first and I went after him. We discovered a distinct flow of water under a low roof and some space beyond. We decided to dive. It took us ages to get the gear down there. We found there was enough draft to show that there was space beyond the cavern, but that most of the channels were heavily silted up which meant excavating and possibly blasting. Then Jamie found another crack, Laura wriggled through it and he followed. That was the last we saw of them. Some rock slipped and closed the crack. But they've found a big cave.'

'Is there water in it?' asked Mrs Crimond anxiously.

'Yes. But there's plenty of air space above it. Jamie says there's enough to last them a day or so.'

Juliet flashed him a warning glance as she noticed the sudden blanching of Mrs Crimond's face and he added hurriedly,

'Of course they'll be out soon. When I left they'd just started blasting.'

'How long is soon?' asked Juliet.

'Oh, another hour or so. It takes a while for the smoke caused by the explosion to clear so that we can see what's happened. And then someone will have to try and worm his way through to them, probably Graham or Lance.'

It was in fact nearly half past ten when Lance walked into the bedroom shared by Mrs Crimond and Juliet to which they had both gone when Mrs Crimond, tired of sitting and waiting, had decided to go to bed. His face and clothes were grimy, but he was smiling and he was closely followed by Jamie, whose clothes and face were even dirtier and whose left arm was in a sling. Behind Jamie came a small equally dirty young woman.

'Mother, this is Laura Penny,' he announced cheerfully. 'I'm going to marry her. She's a fine wee caver.'

His matter-of-fact announcement coming on top of the

hours of waiting and anxiety had the effect of making them all laugh.

'Oh, Jamie, whatever will you do next?' exclaimed his mother, as she searched for a handkerchief in her handbag. 'I've been nearly out of my mind with worry about you while you've been doing your proposing in an underground cave, of all places. Couldn't you have waited until you and Laura had been rescued?'

'No, not really. It was while we were stuck down there that it occurred to me that there was no one I'd rather be trapped with than Laura and that there was no better place for one caver to propose to another than in a cave, with the water swirling round our feet and dripping down on us and the rock glistening in the darkness. Most romantic, don't you think so, Laura?'

The young woman smiled up at him shyly, obviously in agreement.

'I'm sure we're all very pleased to meet you, Laura,' said Mrs Crimond pleasantly, having more or less recovered. 'This is Juliet Grey, my secretary. I'd ask you to sit down, but there's only one chair and Juliet has that ... and your clothes do seem to be a little dirty.'

'Oh, please don't bother,' said Laura in a rush. 'I'm going to have a bath and go straight to bed. I'm so tired, I'd have gone to my room, only Jamie wanted me to meet you.'

'And quite rightly, my dear. I'm very pleased for you both. We'll see you again in the morning, when you're more rested, I hope meanwhile, you'll consider coming back to Castle Ross to stay for a few days, because you'll realise that there'll be no more caving for Jamie this holiday with that arm out of action.'

'I'd like to come very much,' replied Laura, and then escorted by a smiling and obviously triumphant Jamie, who said he would be back after he had washed, she left the room.

'Well, I'm sure I don't know what to say,' sighed Mrs Crimond, lying back against her pillows and closing her eyes.

'It's not often you're at a loss for words,' remarked Lance dryly, and Mrs Crimond's eyes opened immediately and she gave him a wary glance. He had sat down on the edge of Juliet's bed and now he leaned back on one elbow. His hair was dishevelled and he looked rather tired.

'How was the rescue?' asked Juliet curiously, and he glanced at her briefly, impersonally.

'Tough,' he replied. 'The passage we managed to open up was very narrow. They were lucky to get out alive. Mother, I think you should know that Laura is only seventeen.'

'Oh, dear,' sighed Mrs Crimond. 'Then what is she doing here with Jamie, and why has he asked her to marry him?'

'You can ask him that when he comes back.' He rose to his feet. 'I'll go and wash and change too and give him a hand. The doctor in the village says it isn't a break, just a crack in the bone, but I think it should be X-rayed as soon as possible. Jamie's going to be in pain later to-night, especially when the anaesthetic of having got himself engaged has worn off,' he added rather sourly.

He went out of the room. Mrs Crimond's frown of anxiety was once more in evidence.

'Now I wonder what is the matter with him,' she murmured. 'I thought he wasn't in a particularly good mood when he came to see me after you'd come back from sailing.' She gave Juliet one of her disconcertingly sharp glances. 'What did Gareth say to him when he learned that you'd stayed the night on the boat at Dana because of the storm?'

Juliet repeated the exact wording of Gareth's sneer, uneasily aware that Lance's 'bad mood' had begun soon after he had left her sitting alone on the ledge of sandstone in the Cave of the White Rose and had nothing to do with anything Gareth had said. It was something she had done or said which had annoyed him, and for the life of her she couldn't think what it might be.

'Yes, Gareth was quite upset when you didn't return yesterday. In fact he was very irritable when he discovered you'd gone with Lance. Perhaps I should warn you, Juliet, he's very possessive about people he loves. I'm so afraid that he and Lance will quarrel, and that Lance will get fed up with us all and go back to Canada. I couldn't manage without him. You see, he looks after all my business for me.' Mrs Crimond's voice shook with distress, but Juliet had no chance to comfort her because the two brothers returned to the room.

Jamie went straight over to his mother's bed and sat down beside her while Lance propped himself against the wall beside the door. Looking at his dark withdrawn face, Juliet had the impression that he wished heartily that he wasn't there.

'Well, what do you think of Laura, Mother? Isn't she a darling?' asked Jamie, who seemed none the worse for having been trapped underground for hours.

'I shall give you my opinion when I've seen her properly. You might have had more consideration for her bringing her in here looking like that. Poor girl, she must have felt most embarrassed,' replied Mrs Crimond.

'Not Laura. Nothing bothers her,' said Jamie confidently.

'But what is she doing here with you, exploring caves? It's hardly an occupation for a young woman.'

'Why not? Women make grand cavers because they're nimble. It's her hobby just as it's mine.'

Mrs Crimond shuddered delicately.

'I shall never understand the girls of to-day. This urge to do everything that men do, to explore under the ground. So claustrophobic!'

'But it isn't. There's too much to do, to worry about that, isn't there, Lance?'

'I agree,' said Lance. 'Although caving isn't the sort of thing a casual visitor can do. You have to work in groups for safety. How did Laura come to join your group, Jamie?'

Jamie's face changed colour slightly.

'She's the sister of a friend of mine. She showed an interest and I invited her to join the society last year. Graham seemed to have no objections. She's quite mature for her age. But there's the rub. I doubt if her parents will agree to us getting married until she's eighteen.'

'It won't do you any harm to wait.' Lance's suggestion was made casually, but it seemed to strike a spark in Jamie.

'Look who's handing out advice!' he jibed. 'What does a confirmed bachelor like you know about falling in love and wanting to marry?'

'Enough to realise that marriage isn't to be undertaken lightly,' replied Lance equably, impervious to the jibe.

'I'm not undertaking it lightly,' exploded Jamie suddenly. 'I'm older than Gareth was when he married Moira, so I should know my own mind better than he did.'

'And is Laura old enough to know hers?' asked Lance quickly.

'Ach, how I hate your cold-blooded approach to everything! Laura and I are in love and I want to marry her. Waiting won't harm us, but it isn't going to do us any good either,' returned Jamie sulkily.

'Go carefully, dear,' advised his mother gently. 'It won't do to alienate her parents. And since you are several years older than her you mustn't encourage her to defy them. Be engaged for a while in a nice sensible fashion. That way you'll get to know each other a little better, and it will give Laura a chance to grow up. It will also give me a chance to know Laura and for her family to know you.'

Jamie snorted with disgust and standing up began to walk about the cluttered bedroom.

'Families!' he exclaimed scornfully. 'What does family have to do with two people who are in love and want to marry?'

'Quite a lot, dear,' said Mrs Crimond patiently. 'As you should know.'

'Oh yes, I know all right,' Jamie ground out, with a swift underbrowed glance at Lance who was apparently quite uninterested in the conversation. 'But you can be sure, Mother, I shan't let any member of my family come between me and my wife.'

Mrs Crimond's quick almost furtive glance in Lance's

direction and her quiet 'Shush, Jamie!' left Juliet in no doubt that Jamie's last remark was an oblique reference to Lance's association with Moira, and she also looked at him. To her embarrassment she encountered his bright gaze and knew by the faint smile on his face that he had guessed what she was thinking.

'Calm down, Jamie,' he said. 'No one is going to come between you and Laura, and if you're truly in love with each other I'm sure everything will work out to your satisfaction. But why not take Mother's advice? You can't go wrong in observing the conventions in this case.'

'We'll take Laura back to the castle, as I suggested,' put in Mrs Crimond, her frown disappearing as she took delight in making plans. 'She can stay for a few days to recover from what I can only think must have been an unpleasant experience and we'll invite her parents over for next weekend. We'll have a little party, and if they agree, we'll announce your engagement.'

After another uncertain, slightly puzzled, look at Lance Jamie went back to his place on the side of Mrs Crimond's bed and putting an arm round her hugged her.

'Sounds fine, Mother. Just what's needed,' he said.

'We'll invite Janet and Alison over,' said Mrs Crimond, her eyes glowing with excitement.

'Alison Coates?' Jamie was immediately on the alert. 'Where does she fit in?'

'Well, for all your description of Lance as a confirmed bachelor I've been hoping lately that he'll soon announce his decision to marry,' said Mrs Crimond.

Lance raised his eyebrows in an expression of mild surprise.

'I marry? Now why should I do that?' he drawled. 'And whom should I marry?'

The expression on Mrs Crimond's face changed from one of hopefulness to one of intense irritation.

'Alison, of course,' she snapped. 'Now, you can't deny, Lance, that you're interested in her. You've been over to Glenavon nearly every evening since you came to Castle

Ross, and Alison herself told me that she'd met you several times in Glasgow.'

'Which only goes to show what I've often suspected— that women love to exaggerate,' murmured Lance aggravatingly. 'I've been to Glenavon twice since I arrived at Castle Ross. All the other evenings I've been fishing or sailing. Alison and I met twice in Glasgow, once by accident at a cruising club affair, and the second time the day before I drove her home. Hardly enough basis for marriage, to my cold-blooded way of thinking,' he added with a barbed glance in Jamie's direction. 'And hasn't it occurred to you that she might have another interest?'

'I know there was a surgeon at the hospital in the south, but that's all over. She'd made a mistake. She told me herself.'

'I wasn't thinking of him,' said Lance quietly, but his mother didn't seem to hear him, for she went on rather plaintively,

'You and she have been friends for years, off and on...'

'More off than on,' he remarked dryly, 'when you consider that until I bumped into her at that cruising club affair I hadn't seen her since Gareth's wedding.'

'And you'll see more of her,' persisted Mrs Crimond. 'It's always been Janet's and my dearest wish that our two families should be joined by marriage. Oh, the plans we used to make when you and Gareth were boys! It's time you and Alison were married. Neither of you are getting any younger.'

'I can't deny it. I noticed some grey hairs in my head only yesterday morning, and I believe Alison has taken to dyeing her hair,' interrupted Lance wickedly, and Jamie nearly fell off the bed with laughing.

'Give up, Mother,' he advised. 'Can't you see you'll never get him to tell you what he has in mind? If Lance ever marries I'll bet the family will be the last to hear of the arrangement. You're saying all the wrong things.'

'I'm always saying the wrong things to all of you, so it seems,' snapped Mrs Crimond suddenly, as if at the end of her tether. 'Juliet, you've met Alison and you know Lance. Don't you think they're well suited?'

Taken aback by this sudden appeal and attempt to draw her into a family discussion, Juliet went pink as both Jamie and Lance looked at her and waited for her reply. She found it was quite impossible to answer Mrs Crimond's appeal while Lance was there watching her, much as she would have liked to help the older woman in her struggle to get her eldest son to commit himself.

Strangely enough it was Lance who came to her own rescue.

'You don't have to answer that one, Juliet,' he said, and she sent him a grateful glance. 'Aren't you being a little unfair putting Juliet on the spot like that, Mother, when she's met Alison about twice and then only briefly, and as for me...'

'Oh, I know her opinion of you,' interrupted Mrs Crimond crossly. 'She told me that the first time we met, and I'm fast coming to the conclusion that she was right. You're quite infuriating, and why you had to take her sailing with you when I thought you were in agreement with me that it would be ideal if she and Gareth...'

'Mother, Mother!' Jamie's voice was choked with laughter again. 'Please spare Juliet's blushes. This isn't a novel you're writing. You can't arrange marriages in this way. Do you mean to say you asked Juliet to come and work for you in the hopes that Gareth would like her and would marry her?'

'It wasn't my idea that she should come and work for me at all,' said Mrs Crimond unwittingly, 'it was Lance's. But when I saw how Gareth was reacting to her, how much he came out of his shell, the thought did cross my mind and I said as much to Lance—and he didn't disagree ... Now where are you going?'

Lance had already opened the door of the bedroom and was half-way through it. He looked back to answer his mother's sharp demand.

'I've had enough of this rather boring conversation, and

125

it's embarrassing Juliet,' he said coldly. 'I'm going along to the hut which the rest of the cavers are using to have a drink by way of celebration of the finding of the entrance to the main system of caves and the release of Laura and Jamie.'

'Wait for me.' Jamie sprang to his feet.

'Oh, Jamie, you should be in bed, dear, resting,' cautioned Mrs Crimond ineffectually.

'To-morrow,' he grinned down at her. 'I'm not missing a party for anything. You go to sleep. You're the one who's fatigued with worrying needlessly about your awkward brood. Why did you go sailing, Lance? I thought you were coming here on Saturday. I'd told everyone you were coming,' he said as he walked over to the door.

'I gave in to impulse, something I rarely do, and as you can guess by the uproar it's caused, I'm fast regretting it,' replied Lance. His cold glance drifted to Juliet who was looking at him with suddenly troubled and accusing eyes. 'I'd ask you to come to the party, Juliet, but as things stand at present between you and Gareth such an invitation might be misunderstood,' he remarked acidly. His glance passed on to his mother and he inclined his head with an affectionate grin. 'Good night, matriarch. Your suggestion concerning Alison is interesting. Maybe I'll think about it.'

He closed the door behind him and Jamie, and Mrs Crimond let out an exasperated sigh.

'Was there ever anyone so aggravating!' she complained, putting a hand to her head. 'I'm very much afraid I've said the wrong thing, as Jamie pointed out. I should have had more sense than to mention marriage to Lance. He's always been touchy about it, ever since Gareth married Moira. But I'd hoped that he'd got over that disappointment by now. After all, twelve years is a long time and Moira has been dead almost one. Oh, what a difficult situation it was, almost nightmarish.'

'In what way?' asked Juliet.

'Both my sons in love with the same woman. I've told you Lance brought Moira home, but Gareth fell in love with her at first sight and it was soon obvious that she preferred him to Lance. Then Lance went off to Canada, and while he was away Gareth and Moira decided to get married. Invitations were sent out, with one to Lance of course. We didn't know he was coming until he turned up at the last minute and told Gareth he was a fool to go through with the ceremony just before the poor boy was to leave for the church. Robert was furious with him, as you can imagine, and there were the usual fireworks. I can still remember the way Lance came to me and pleaded with me to stop the wedding. I could do nothing, so he went to Moira's home and tried to prevent her from going to the church. Quite naturally she didn't listen to him. He left and went back to Canada as soon as the ceremony was over, and I've never known since then what he'd really been thinking or feeling.'

After she had gone to bed and had switched out the bedside lamp Juliet lay awake for a long time, aware of Mrs Crimond's restlessness in the other bed.

She agreed with the other woman that Lance's answers to her suggestion that he might marry Alison eventually had been aggravating. He had obviously no intention of allowing his mother or anyone else to know how he felt about the red-haired woman whom he had known off and on for so long. But two things had been confirmed that evening. Lance had been in love with Moira and he had lost her to Gareth. Yet in the end wasn't it possible that he had not lost her at all? That they had picked up where they had left off when he had returned from Canada to find Gareth crippled? It was that part about which Juliet couldn't be sure, and it was the part which bothered her the most for some reason. She couldn't bear to think that possibly Lance had deceived his brother.

She turned on her side and tried to sleep. But just as she was growing drowsy the other vital piece of information she had learned that evening and which had confirmed an earlier suspicion pricked her into wakefulness again to worry and tantalise her. Now she knew for certain that

127

Lance had brought her to Castle Ross deliberately to carry out his boast that he could find another wife for Gareth, just as he had found the first one.

CHAPTER FIVE

NEXT morning Mrs Crimond didn't feel well. She lay limp and apathetic against her pillows, her blue eyes drawn and shadowed, her thin ascetic face pale and haggard.

'It's no good, Juliet. I can't possibly travel back to-day,' she said. 'It would be too much on top of yesterday's journey and two very anxious nights. Lance will have to make arrangements for us to stay another night here. I'm sure Mrs Robertson won't mind if I keep to this room to-day until I feel more rested. I won't have any breakfast, just a glass of milk. Perhaps you'd like to phone Gareth again and tell him why we won't be back, otherwise he'll worry about you. I hope you don't mind putting in the day by yourself. Did I disturb you during the night?'

'No, I was awake anyway, part of the time. Too much excitement yesterday, I expect,' said Juliet, trying to be cheerful and alert.

'Then a nice quiet day won't do you any harm, either, nor Jamie and Laura for that matter.' Mrs Crimond frowned again. 'It was past two o'clock when Jamie and Lance came back. I heard them, for all they tried to creep past the door.'

Juliet had heard them too, so when she went into the dining room she was surprised to see Lance already there, alone, eating his breakfast. She explained to him about his mother.

'I half expected it,' he replied coolly. 'She was very tired, and when she's like that she gets over-excited and talks too much, then she can't sleep.'

'No thanks to you,' she rebuked him sharply, knowing that it had been his remarks concerning Alison which had kept his mother wakeful. But she might as well have saved

128

her breath, because he merely gave her a cold, slightly haughty glance which dismissed her comment as unnecessary.

'Jamie isn't feeling too good this morning either,' he said, 'so I was going to suggest we delayed our return until tomorrow. Won't you sit down,' he added politely. 'The table is set for two and the waitress should be back soon.'

He was firmly entrenched behind that film of ice which she had noticed yesterday whenever he had spoken to her, and once again she wondered what she had done or said to annoy him.

'I'd like to make a phone call first,' she replied hastily, thinking it was a good excuse to avoid having to have breakfast alone with him again.

'Gareth?' he enquired accurately, and looked at his watch. 'Too early. He won't be up yet, so you'd better wait. Sit down.'

She was obeying his curt order before she realised it, lowering herself slowly into the seat opposite to him, watching him pour tea into one of the cups set on the table. He pushed a full cup across to her.

'You look as if you need it. Did you have a sleepless night too, no thanks to me?' he asked sardonically.

How unkind he was, deliberately and unpleasantly unkind. He went out of his way to torment people. Was it a form of self-defence to keep everyone at a distance so that they wouldn't enquire about his real feelings? Was it because he had once cared deeply about someone and had been badly hurt, and didn't want that to happen again?

Juliet stirred her tea reflectively, thinking of what she had learned about him from his mother the previous evening.

'You're doing it again,' he cautioned crisply. 'Wondering about something which is none of your business.'

She met his clear cold gaze across the table, but this time she didn't let herself be put off by his apparent omniscience regarding her thoughts.

'You can't stop me from wondering. Mysteries have

129

always intrigued me,' she replied.

The film of ice was cracked for a moment as he laughed at her.

'But there's no mystery. You've been reading too many of Tess's books,' he jeered.

She shook her head and her pale hair glinted in the sunlight which poured in through the window near which they were sitting.

'No, I haven't, and I don't agree with you. There is a mystery. You are the mystery.'

For a brief moment he looked disconcerted, then his face stiffened and the crack in the ice closed up.

'So I'm a mystery and you'd like to solve me,' he drawled. 'Sorry, but it's against my nature to offer any clues. I guess your interest is well-meant, but I think I've warned you before not to concern yourself with anything beyond the job you're paid to do.'

'A job which didn't exist until you invented it,' she retorted.

'Of course it did,' he countered imperturbably. 'Just because my mother says it wasn't her idea that you should work for her that doesn't mean to say she didn't need a secretary—companion. She's always needed one, but she was hopeless at choosing the right sort of person for the job, so this time I did it for her. From all accounts you're very satisfactory except for an unfortunate tendency on your part to be curious about matters which are not your concern.' He paused, then added threateningly, 'Keep off the grass, Juliet. You're not welcome.'

The sharp rebuff hurt far more than it should have done, and she was trying to deal with the emotional upheaval he had just caused when the young waitress came in and apologised for keeping her waiting. Juliet gave her order in a low voice, then turned away to look out of the window because to her annoyance her eyes were filling with tears. How stupid to behave like this because a man she didn't like very much had rebuffed her! She felt like a child who, reaching out for and wanting friendship, had been rejected.

A chair leg scraped against the polished wooden floor as he rose to his feet.

'I'll leave you to have your breakfast in peace and go and see Tess,' he said, and his voice sounded oddly flat and dull, causing her to look at him. He had half turned away ready to move towards the door when a thought seemed to strike him and he turned back. His eyes narrowed as they observed the slight droop to the corners of her sensitive mouth and the sheen of tears in her eyes.

'What are you going to do with yourself to-day?' he asked abruptly.

'I thought I'd go for a walk,' she muttered.

He leaned against the back of the chair he had just vacated and stared at the table as if deep in thought. A lock of hair slid forward on to his forehead and he pushed it back impatiently, then rubbed the side of his face with his fingers. Juliet had the impression that he was hesitating about something, and was surprised. She had never had reason to consider him to be a hesitant person before.

'Would you like to see where the caves are?' he asked suddenly.

'Yes, I would.'

'I'm going up there this morning to help bring back equipment. With Jamie and Laura out of action they're short-handed. You could come with me, if you like.'

If she liked. It was the same sort of invitation he'd issued on Saturday morning when he'd asked her to go sailing, and this time she was more suspicious.

'Are you sure you won't regret the impulse which prompts you to invite me?' she asked with a touch of acidity.

His glance was lightning bright and she braced herself for another rebuff.

'I might ... later. But that's my affair, not yours,' he said tersely. 'Do you want to come?'

'Yes, I do, if you're sure such an outing wouldn't be beyond the limits of the job I'm paid to do,' she replied coolly, and then wilted visibly when she saw his face darken ominously. But he didn't retort. Instead the film of ice cracked suddenly and he smiled at her.

'The rose has thorns,' he mocked, coming round the table to stand beside her. 'I deserved both of those pricks. Yes, I suppose I am behaving inconsistently and that the outing to the caves is beyond the limits of your job just as going sailing was, but I thought perhaps you'd prefer to see something of the countryside instead of moping about here all day on your own. Would you?'

In the face of this surprising show of consideration for her well-being she couldn't help smiling back at him.

'Yes, I would very much,' she said.

'Then I shall see you in the entrance hall in about half an hour. That should give you time to eat and to phone Gareth. It might be a good idea to tell him where you're going and with whom, because if he doesn't hear it from you and someone else should tell him he might think you were being unnecessarily secretive and get some funny ideas. Oh, and one more warning. I'd appreciate it if you didn't try to solve mysteries on the way there and back. Do you understand?'

For a moment they stared at each other; sea-green eyes puzzled and a little hurt; grey eyes wary and watchful. Then Juliet inclined her head and whispered,

'I understand.'

Later when she phoned Gareth his voice sounded warm and welcoming as he greeted her, and he chattered away happily, telling her about the work he was doing that morning and saying that he missed her very much.

'I'll give you three guesses why,' he teased gently.

'There isn't time,' she stammered as she noticed Lance walk past the kiosk in the entrance of the hotel and cock an enquiring eye in her direction. 'We've already had more than three minutes.'

'Lance is paying, so why should we care?' he chuckled. 'Tell me why I'm missing you.'

'Because you want some typing done.'

'Right first time. So make sure you come back tomorrow without fail.'

'I must go now,' she said hurriedly. 'Lance is waiting.'

'Why?'

'We're going up to the cave to help bring down equipment.'

'You don't have to go with him.'

'No, but I'd like to see the caves.'

'Don't go,' he said urgently.

'Why shouldn't I?'

'Because you might get lost, or have an accident,' he said seriously.

'No, I won't. I shall be quite safe.'

'That's what you think!'

'Gareth, what's the matter? You're not making sense.'

'Oh, nothing. It was just a thought I had. Goodbye, Juliet.'

It was impossible to hide the puzzlement she felt as she stepped out of the kiosk, and Lance's all-seeing glance noted it. His mouth took on a sardonic curve as he remarked,

'I gather Gareth was on form. Shall we go now?'

She nodded and he led the way out into the clear sparkling morning air.

The first part of the journey to the caves was along a rough road to a lonely white cottage set on the moors at the back of the village. As they drove along, rising steadily higher and higher, Lance pointed out the hut which was the cavers' headquarters and which had once been a deerstalker's bothy. He also drew her attention to the isolated mountain peaks of the area which protruded above a wilderness of low hillocks and innumerable small lochs. Most of these mountains possessed very definite shapes, and Lance told her that one of them always reminded him of a fairy castle, which had been pictured in one of his childhood books, perched on the top of steep slopes, and that another seemed to resemble a sugar loaf because its greyish quartzite boulders sparkled like sugar in the bright light.

And gazing silently at the two mountains Juliet was surprised again that he was capable of such a fantasy.

When they reached the cottage Lance parked the car beside the Land-Rover used by the cavers and went to the house to arrange to borrow the two small horses which were grazing on the hillside at the back. They were known as garrons, he informed Juliet, a species of horse indigenous to Scotland which were nowadays used mostly for deerstalking.

'Have you ever ridden a horse before?' he asked, noticing that she was eyeing the stocky, long-maned animals with a certain amount of apprehension.

'No. Do I have to?'

'Like sailing a boat, it's an experience you shouldn't miss. It's about four miles from here to the caves over rough moorland. We'll ride there and walk back leading the horses, which will be loaded with gear. I'll help you up on to its back.'

'No saddle?' she queried.

'Bareback for fun,' he replied with a grin. 'Come on, there's nothing to be afraid of. They're quite docile and used to carrying novices.'

She tried hard to heave herself up on to the back of the smaller of the two animals, but couldn't quite make it, and in the end allowed Lance to lift her up on to its back. He showed her how to hold the reins, then turned away to mount the other horse. He was far too big for it and presented a sight which tickled Juliet's sense of humour and sent her off into fits of giggles.

'What's so funny?' he demanded.

'You are, on that horse. You look like a giant on a pony. Your feet almost touch the ground.'

'They do,' he replied, showing her. 'These horses used to be ridden by Highlanders to cross country in the past. They're capable of carrying a person for miles no matter what his height or weight. Are you ready?'

'I think so,' she said dubiously.

He turned his horse and it trotted out through the gate of

the yard on to the moorland path. Juliet tried to turn her horse to follow him, but it remained stubbornly in the same place. She pulled on the reins, clucked her tongue, but it didn't move, except to lower its head and start nibbling at a tuft of grass. Lance looked round, saw her predicament and came back.

'Kick with your heels and it'll move,' he instructed.

She did, and the horse moved off obediently at a far faster pace than she had anticipated. It had a peculiar rocking motion and she could feel the action of its back muscles beneath her. She kicked again, hoping to make it go faster so that she could catch up with Lance, and it broke into a lurching trot. Not being used to riding, Juliet didn't know how to move when a horse trotted, so she bumped up and down on its back, feeling sure that at any minute she would slide off sideways.

When she did go, it wasn't sideways. The horse stopped suddenly and she shot off over its lowered head, did an unexpected somersault and landed on her back in a bed of springy bog myrtle.

Bewildered, bruised and breathless, she lay and blinked at the sunny sky for several seconds, panic-stricken in case she'd broken any bones, remembering Gareth's concern about her, and his insistence that she shouldn't go with Lance. Then the thud of hooves on the ground told her that Lance was on his way back to see what had happened and she struggled on to her knees.

'What happened?' he asked, slipping off his horse and coming to help her to her feet.

'The silly thing stopped and I fell off, that's all,' she replied shakily as she tested each leg gingerly before putting her full weight on either of them. Looking up as he released her arm, she saw amusement lurking in his eyes. He was laughing at her because she couldn't ride just as he'd laughed at her when she had got drenched with spray on the boat. She was suddenly angry. 'I could have hurt myself badly,' she accused hotly. 'I could have broken an arm or a leg, or fallen on my head and cracked my skull and

135

died.'

'And that would have taught me a lesson, because accidents happen to people when they're with me. Isn't that how it goes?' he put in coldly. 'I'm surprised Gareth didn't warn you against coming with me when you phoned him.'

'He did,' she retorted.

'Yet you came.'

'Yes—after all, I'm not Moira.'

Her hand went to her mouth and her eyes widened with dismay as she saw his face go pale and a strange expression, it could have been pain, flicker in his eyes.

'No, you're not Moira,' he agreed quietly. 'She knew how to ride.' Just as she'd known how to sail, how to ski, how to climb hills, how to do everything, thought Juliet miserably. How could she, who could only type, possibly compete with such a paragon? And on top of that question came another —why would she want to compete?

Confused and shaken, she looked round at the seemingly never-ending moorland where the heather was already purple, at the distant hills shimmering silver-grey in the sunlight. It was a beautiful morning and she had started out with high hopes thinking that perhaps this might be one of those perfect days, a day to remember. A big golden bird appeared high in the sky flapping its wings lazily. Then gliding on a current of air it swooped downwards and disappeared beyond the edge of the moor.

'A golden eagle,' murmured Lance, half to himself. 'Probably after a mountain hare, or a grouse.'

Juliet shuddered. 'Poor little prey!' she mourned.

'You feel an affinity with it, perhaps,' he taunted, swinging round to look at her. 'Only the other day you compared me to an eagle. You know, considering your opinion of me I'm surprised you wanted to come to-day. Well, do you want to go on or would you rather go back and sit in the car until I return with the others?'

For the second time that morning tears were very near. Her perfect day had already been spoiled and possibly would be remembered only for hard words, but she knew

136

she couldn't bear to stay and sit in his car while he rode on to the caves. She had to go with him. She had to take up the challenge that going anywhere with him offered.

'I want to go on,' she replied.

'Then get on the garron.' He helped her up on to the horse's back and put the reins in her hand. 'This time, stay put,' he ordered. 'And don't try to hurry. We have all day to get there and back. I'll ride beside you so that I can keep an eye on you. That way we'll avoid any accidents, I hope.'

There were no more incidents and soon she began to enjoy the ride in the clear mountain air. The only sounds were the perpetual chuckle of a burn as it rushed down the hillside over pale stones, and the occasional mournful cry of a bird.

They kept close to the burn following its course through the narrow glen it had made. As he had promised, Lance kept beside her, occasionally reaching out a hand to grasp her horse's bridle to guide it round some obstacle he had seen and she hadn't. He spoke only once to point out the change in the landscape as the bog myrtle and sedge gave way to short green grass and small bushes with clumps of hazel and mountain ash trees. The hills had lost their rock-bun shape and were sharper-edged, and she recognised a similarity to the area around the Cauldron on the Castle Ross estate. This was part of the big limestone thrust about which Jamie had told her on that day, so long ago now it seemed, when he had driven her from Glasgow to Loch Moy.

The burn disappeared underground where a long fissure made a ragged gash in a hillside.

'This is the outlet of this particular stream,' said Lance as they paused to look down into the deep crack. 'We'll find the others higher up the hill.'

After a fairly steep climb up the craggy hillside they came to the place where the burn went underground on its way down from its source. Graham and his helpers were lounging beside the deep gash eating their lunches. Nearby three more garrons stood already loaded with the sub-aqua diving gear which the cavers had been using.

The cavers greeted Lance cheerfully and stared curiously at the pale-haired girl whom he helped down from her horse.

'I see you've brought a fairy princess with you this morning,' said Graham with a grin. 'Good morning, Miss Grey. Have you come to see the scene of yesterday's little drama? If you'd like to be stepping this way I'll show you where we had to go and you'll hear the roaring of the water as it falls over a step of rock.'

He led her to the edge of the deep fissure which was overhung by small bushes and creeping plants. It was wide and dark, and far below she could hear the sound of water.

'This is where we first tried to gain entry last summer,' explained Graham, 'but it led only to an impassable water trap, something like the one you'll find below a wash-hand basin. So we dug a pit between the accumulated scree and debris and the rock face over there until we found a crack.' He pointed to the opposite side of the fissure. 'That's the crack which Laura was able to enter last week.'

'But it's only a few inches high!' exclaimed Juliet. 'However did she get in?'

'Nine and a half inches, to be exact,' replied Graham. 'And she got in by lying on her back and wriggling about like a snake. Anyway, she was able to tell us that after a few feet it widened out into a small cave where there was another crack about seven inches high. We were all able to wriggle into that crack over there, but the seven-inch one defeated us and that's when we had to start blasting, and the trouble began. But at least we know now that our first guesses were right and that there's a big cave system under this hill which will rival that of Cnoc na Uamh.'

'Where is that?'

'A few miles away.'

'No progress this morning?' asked Lance, coming to join them.

138

'No. We need a bigger party to do some digging. At the moment the system is only passable for divers. We'll have to find another entrance. We explored some more potholes this morning, but we miss Laura and Jamie, so we'll postpone investigation for another year. Unless you'd care to try and wriggle into one of the cracks and report back some information to us, Miss Grey?' said Graham, turning to smile at her.

'Now go easy, Graham,' warned Lance, and Juliet felt his hand grip her elbow and pull her back gently from the edge of the crack. 'I brought her to see the place and to help with the humping back of the equipment, not as a replacement for Laura. She isn't my property, so I have to take great care she doesn't get lost or hurt or there'll be hell to pay back at Castle Ross.'

Graham's shrewd grey eyes flicked from Lance's face to Juliet's and back again.

'Aye, I can imagine, but there are other ways of getting lost or hurt than falling down a pothole,' he murmured obscurely. 'If you were my property, Miss Grey, I wouldn't be letting you roam the countryside with this rogue.' He jerked a thumb in the direction of Lance.

'Then what would you do?' asked Juliet, at once amused and fascinated by the strange turn in the conversation.

'I'd keep you locked up until he'd passed by.'

'I'd no idea you had such a medieval outlook on life,' said Lance with a laugh. 'Now, tell us what you'd like us to load on to the garrons and after we've eaten our lunch we'll start back.'

Juliet ate the packed lunch which Lance had brought from the hotel sitting beside the deep chasm. The noonday sun shone down out of a cloudless sky, and the only sounds were the muffled roar of the hidden water and the desultory conversation of the men. Feeling relaxed, Juliet leaned back on her elbows and gazed back down the glen up which she and Lance had recently come.

Difficult of access, devoid of any habitation, the place had a wild romantic beauty to which sunshine and shadow

139

added their serenity and mystery. Amongst such scenery it wasn't difficult to take seriously Graham's strange remarks about fairy princesses and rogues.

Her gaze slid down from contemplation of the summit of the hills to Lance where he sprawled on the ground beside Graham listening to the other man's slow voice. Her glance lingered on the strong, bold features of his face outlined against the pale rock behind him. Certainly he looked more of a rogue than a knight in shining armour. She assumed that Graham's description was based on a fairly close knowledge of Lance and it was the sort of thing that could only be said to a friend. Odd to find that Lance had a close friend. He seemed such a loner, a person apart, even from his family, difficult to know and understand—an uncomfortable person to have around, as Jamie had once said.

And if, as Mrs Crimond and apparently Lance himself wished, she married Gareth, Lance would be her brother-in-law.

The thought alarmed her and she sat up suddenly, clasping her arms around her knees. Up here in the hills of the north-west Gareth seemed very far away and insubstantial and she didn't want to think about marrying him.

A shadow came between her and the sun. She knew at once who it was and glanced up warily to meet the enigmatic glitter of light grey eyes.

'Graham thinks you should see Cnoc na Uamh while you're here, so we'll go round that way instead of going back the way we came,' Lance said. 'It's a long way and it will take us most of the afternoon to get back to the cottage.'

She looked round in surprise. While she had been lazing and thinking the garrons had been loaded and the other cavers had already set off down the glen.

To reach the Hill of Caves they had to walk round the shoulder of the hill in a north-westerly direction, leading the loaded garrons behind them. On the way Juliet talked to Graham and she learned that he was a teacher of science in an Edinburgh school, and that he was married and had two children.

'Don't you bring them with you when you come caving?' she asked.

'Ach, no. It's my hobby, not theirs. And one advantage of being a teacher is that I can have a holiday with them and then take a few days off to go caving.'

'How long have you been caving?'

'About ten years, perhaps more.' He half-turned to ask Lance who was walking behind them, 'How long since we spent that holiday in South Wales?'

'More than twelve. The grey is beginning to show in your hair too,' joked Lance.

'What little I have of it,' laughed Graham. 'Aye, that was the beginning of it. We went potholing amongst the Welsh hills with a group from the University. It made a change from cruising in the Western Isles in someone else's yacht, which was our usual occupation during the summer months, and the bug bit me down there. Two years later a book was published about the underground caves of Scotland and that clinched the matter. I formed a society, with Lance's support. We got some experience with other groups down in Derbyshire, then we came up here, because although the main area of caves have been known for some time they haven't all been properly explored.'

Soon they reached the arched openings in Cnoc na Uamh which Juliet duly admired. Graham pointed out that most of the stalactite and stalagmite formations, the long needle-like formations hanging from the roofs or protruding upwards from the floors, had mostly been removed by casual visitors to the caves, an act of vandalism which he deplored, as such formations were rare in Scotland.

When they set off down the hillside, going south this time, Juliet walked again with Graham, with whom she was on very good terms by now, and asked him if he knew that there was an underground stream near Castle Ross.

'Yes, but Lance says the system isn't very big and that there would have to be a lot of blasting done, and he doesn't want that. Have you seen it?'

141

'Maree took me to see it.'

'She's Gareth's child?'

'Yes. Do you know her?'

'I haven't seen her since she was a wee bairn. I knew her mother. Fearless as they come. Lance says the girl is very like her. A hard time her father will be having keeping her in order, if that's the case,' Graham observed dryly. 'You know how her mother died?'

'I know that there was an accident of some sort, that's all.'

'Aye, when she was skiing abroad. She was warned not to go out, but she insisted on going when there'd been an avalanche warning. She was very wilful, was Moira, and I know of only one person who could keep her in her place.' He jerked his head backwards in the direction of Lance, who appeared to be in no hurry to catch up with them.

'But if that was so why wasn't he able to stop her from going out when there was a warning?' asked Juliet.

Graham flashed her a surprised glance.

'How could he? He wasn't there.'

'But ... but ...' Juliet felt as if she were groping in a fog even though the day was very clear. 'I've been led to believe that he was.'

'Led to believe is right,' remarked Graham caustically. 'May I ask by whom?'

'Gareth. I heard him say that if he hadn't let Moira go with Lance that last time she'd be alive now.'

Graham was silent as he turned this piece of information over in his mind,

'So that's the way of it,' he murmured at last. 'It would be interesting to find out who has been misleading whom, and perhaps we'll never know because Lance isn't one to discuss family or personal affairs. But I'm willing to bet he wasn't with Moira.'

'But he often took her out, I've heard Mrs Crimond say so. He thought he was helping Gareth when he was unable to get about because of the paralysis in his leg.'

'Curiouser and curiouser. There seems to be a wee bit of

a mystery here, don't you think?'

'Why do you say that?' she asked sharply.

'I knew Moira quite well. As I've said, she was wilful and headstrong. If she wanted to go anywhere she would go. She wouldn't wait for anyone to invite her,' he said with an air of authority. 'I also know Lance better than most people do, and I can't believe he would invite her to go anywhere with him because he disliked her.'

'Disliked her? Oh, but Mrs Crimond told me that he was in love with her and was very disappointed when she married Gareth.'

'Aye, it looked that way at the time and maybe he was attracted to her for a while, after all she was interested in all out-of-door activities just as he was, but he soon forgot her when he went to Canada. It was when he came back and saw what she'd done to Gareth that he began to dislike her. You see, although it may not be very apparent, because he isn't a demonstrative man, Lance has very great affection for the members of his family. For them he would do anything, as he would for anyone he loved, and so...'

'Sharing secrets already?'

Lance had caught up with them, and Juliet glanced with alarm at him, realising that in the last few minutes she had been very concerned with something outside the limits of her job. But the mockery in his eyes was directed at Graham, not at her.

'You certainly have a way with the lasses, Graham,' he taunted with a grin. 'You must tell me how you do it some time.'

'Nothing to it,' replied the tall Scot imperturbably. 'When a lass is like a fairy princess and her heart is in the right place a man can't help confiding in her. Anyway, where have you been loitering?'

'The garron got a stone in its hoof and I've been removing it. It's limping a bit, so I think I'll unload some of the gear. I'll leave it here and perhaps Eric or Morley can come back and pick it up.'

The limping horse slowed down their progress because

Graham kept pace with Lance and Juliet could do no less. The conversation concerned mostly plans for caving the following year when Graham hoped that Lance would join the expedition.

When they reached the cottage they found Eric and Morley waiting there, and Graham sent Eric to get the gear which had been left behind before walking over to the car with Juliet and Lance.

'This isn't the end of our acquaintance Juliet,' he said with a smile. 'There's a *ceilidh* on in the village hall to-night and I'm inviting you to come to it.'

'A *ceilidh*?'

'Aye, a get-together of everyone in the village and the outlying district as well as people who are on holiday up here. There'll be some Scottish dancing and some singing, and I'm thinking you'd like it. We had a fine wee party last night, but it was strictly all-male. To-night I'm making up for that by asking you to come along. Will you?'

'I'd love to,' smiled Juliet.

'Tut, tut,' mocked Lance. 'What would Helen say if she knew?'

'She'd approve,' retorted his friend. 'If she were here she'd be doing the inviting herself and telling you you're a proud stubborn oaf who can't see any farther than the end of his nose.'

There was a funny silence as Lance stared at his friend and Graham returned the stare with narrowed eyes.

'Has it ever occurred to you that perhaps I can see farther, very clearly, and that I'm trying to avoid complications?' returned Lance icily.

'And making more as you do,' countered Graham.

'Watch it, Graham!' It was a haughtily uttered threat.

'All right, it's none of my business, but I'm surprised at you, and it's time you started putting yourself first and be damned to your brother.'

'Come on, Juliet,' said Lance. 'We'll leave this madman now, and hope that he'll have recovered from the touch of the sun he seems to have by the time the *ceilidh* starts.'

As the car bumped down the rough road towards the village Juliet caught sight of the mountain, which looked like a fairy castle on the edge of a precipice; a castle where the princess would lie sleeping until the prince came to wake her with a kiss ...

'Well, was it a good day?' asked Lance abruptly, breaking into her daydream. Roused from her contemplation of the mountain, she glanced sideways at him. He was frowning, and the creases from the corners of his nose to the corners of his mouth were very marked.

'Yes, it was, thank you,' she said primly, thinking she must keep the conversation cool and conventional. 'Graham is very interesting. I learned a lot from him.'

'I bet you did,' he replied savagely, and she looked at him again. Was it possible that he was angry, really angry? Even as she looked at him he jammed on the brakes and the car came to a lurching, crunching stop at the side of the road.

He turned in his seat to face her.

'What did you learn?' he rapped.

Still confused by Graham's remarks about Moira which had given her a totally new view of Lance's relationship with his late sister-in-law, she shrank back against the door of the car, away from the anger which glittered in his eyes.

'I learned about stalactites and stalagmites,' she quavered, and heard him swear rather wearily.

'That isn't what I meant, and you know it, mystery-solver. What else did you learn?'

His anger had passed as quickly as it had blown up. He turned away from her and leaned his arms on the steering wheel and resting his chin on them closed his eyes, and for the first time since she had known him he seemed to Juliet to be thoroughly human; a man who did what he did because he was prompted by pride, affection, anger, and immediately all her fear and dislike of him faded to nothing.

'I learned that you disliked Moira for what she did to Gareth,' she answered quietly.

He didn't move a muscle.

145

'Is that all?' he said warily.

'Yes.'

'I thought I'd told you not to try and solve any mysteries.'

'I didn't. We were talking about Maree and Graham asked if I knew how her mother had died and I told him I didn't . . .'

'And he decided to fill you in. Very obliging of him, I'm sure,' he said sarcastically. 'Well, for your information Graham knows nothing about the circumstances surrounding Moira's death. No one knows here, except me.'

'But Gareth . . .'

'He knows what I decided to tell him. She went skiing with me. There was an avalanche warning, but she insisted on going out. There was nothing I could do to stop her. That's the story, Juliet, and I'd be glad if you'd leave it that way, and stop probing.'

'And if I don't stop probing, what will you do?' she couldn't resist challenging.

'I don't know, but you can be sure it won't be pleasant,' he grated.

'But I don't understand,' she blurted rebelliously. 'Why did you lie to Gareth . . .'

He moved quickly. His hand stung her delicate skin as he slapped it across her mouth so that she couldn't say any more.

'I warned you,' he hissed. 'Do you want to stay at Castle Ross?'

'I'm not sure that I can stay now,' she answered, as he removed his hand and slumped back into his seat.

'That is of course entirely up to you,' he said coldly as he switched on the ignition, started the engine and manoeuvred the car back on to the road, and the rest of the drive back to the hotel was made in uncomfortable silence.

When they reached the hotel Juliet let herself out of the car with a muffled word of thanks and hurried inside. Her one aim was to be by herself to give way to the tears which were threatening. But she had forgotten she was sharing a

146

room with Mrs Crimond and her face registered her disappointment at finding the room occupied by that lady, who
was sitting in front of the dressing table attending to her
hair.

Too late Juliet tried to cover up. Mrs Crimond had
noticed her reflection in the mirror and swung round to look
directly at her.

'Why, Juliet dear, whatever is the matter? You're quite
pale and distressed-looking. There hasn't been ...? Lance is
all right?'

'Yes, we're both all right,' whispered Juliet. 'There's
nothing the matter,' and promptly burst into tears.

With a quick impulsive movement Mrs Crimond was out
of her chair and putting her arms round Juliet.

'Oh, my dear, what is it? Come and sit down and tell
me.'

Sitting on the side of her bed, Juliet tried vainly to recover, taking her handkerchief and blowing her nose and
wiping her eyes.

'It's so silly,' she hiccupped. 'Nothing to cry about really,
only ...'

'Only what? You'd better tell me. Has that abominable
son of mine done something to upset you?'

'No, I mean, yes. Well, he had every right to say what he
did, but ...' Fresh tears made it impossible for her to continue.

'But he could have said it more pleasantly, I know,'
sighed Mrs Crimond. 'It's the Crimond in him. Neither his
father nor his grandfather were in the least tactful.'

'He said I must stop trying to solve mysteries.'

'What mystery are you trying to solve? Something to do
with the caves?' Mrs Crimond sounded completely bewildered.

'No. It's difficult to explain, and it's possible I'm imagining it. It's to do with Lance and Gareth and Moira, and
now it's been made more complicated by what Graham Lee
said this afternoon.'

'What did he say?' asked Mrs Crimond.

'He said he didn't believe that Lance was with Moira on that skiing trip when she was killed. He said that Lance disliked Moira.'

'But he loved her. That was the trouble and has always been the trouble. It's that which has soured the relationship between him and Gareth,' exclaimed Mrs Crimond.

'That's what I thought—not because anyone told me but just from observing.'

'And adding two and two together from the odd conversations which occasionally take place,' said Mrs Crimond sympathetically. 'Yes, I can understand, because that's all I've ever been able to do. Lance has never confided in me. He isn't the type. And although Gareth makes a pretence of doing so, I know he withholds things. I've never really expected them to tell me everything, believing that once your children grow up you mustn't expect them to come running to you with their problems, but that hasn't stopped me from wishing secretly that they would. Oh, dear, what a muddle, but I'm sure you know what I mean, Juliet.'

Juliet nodded, smiling a rather wobbly smile. Talking to Mrs Crimond was helping her immeasurably. It helped to know that someone else who was close to the two eldest Crimonds was just as puzzled by their behaviour.

'But on what grounds does Graham base his idea that Lance disliked Moira?' asked Mrs Crimond.

'He seems to know him very well. They've been friends for years.'

'You surprise me. I'd no idea that Lance had any close friends. Did he tell you anything else?'

'Only that Lance is very fond of his family and will do anything to help them.'

'That I know to be true in my case and possibly in Jamie's, and even though he and his father argued many times he didn't hesitate to come home when Robert was ill and I believe he was sincerely upset when his father died. It used to be true also in the case of Gareth, especially when they were boys. Being the stronger of the two Lance tended

148

to protect Gareth when they were at school, but lately I would say his attitude has fallen far short of affection, because there have been times when he's been downright unkind.'

'I know,' said Juliet. 'But why?'

'Did Graham tell you why Lance disliked Moira?' asked Mrs Crimond shrewdly.

'He was just saying that it was because of what she did to Gareth when Lance came up and accused us of sharing secrets, so of course Graham didn't say any more. But later when we were coming back here Lance was annoyed because he suspected Graham and I had been discussing him, and he said ... he warned me ...' Juliet gulped and swallowed more tears.

'I see,' murmured Mrs Crimond, her eyes vacant as she stared at Juliet without actually seeing her, obviously thinking hard. 'There is something which Lance doesn't want Gareth to know and he's afraid that if you find out about it you'll tell Gareth. There is a mystery after all, and I think Graham may be able to help us. What did Moira do to Gareth? I've no idea, apart from the fact that I suspected they weren't very happy during the last few years of their marriage. I wonder how we can find out?'

'We?' queried Juliet.

'Yes. You must see, dear, that I've been very troubled by the deteriorating relationship between Lance and Gareth, but by nature I tend to avoid anything unpleasant, so I've not questioned either of them. And then Gareth has never uttered a word of criticism of Moira. As far as he's concerned she was perfect. You must find out from Graham what he was going to tell you. Between now and to-morrow morning, when we'll be leaving, you'll have to pump him, Juliet.'

Juliet had no doubts that she would be able to question Graham further about Moira when she attended the *ceilidh*. The thought of going to the party cheered her up and she felt much better when she had changed into a multi-coloured gathered skirt which sported a deep frill round its hem and topped it with a simple full-sleeved blouse. She tied her pale hair back from her face into a high ponytail from which it fanned out on her shoulders.

As she walked with him to the village hall Graham explained to her that the social gathering which would take place that evening was not a *ceilidh* in the true sense of the word, because that was usually an informal spontaneous affair held in someone's house. But the event that evening had been organised by the proprietors of the hotel for the entertainment of the many summer visitors to the area who usually came from overseas and who wished to see a little local colour. There would be a four-piece band and local singers would show off their talent in singing Gaelic ballads and other well-known Scottish songs. The dancing would be varied, but there would be a preponderance of Scottish dances.

'They're very enjoyable when you get used to them. As long as you have a strong sense of rhythm and remember eight beats to every bar you'll be all right, because the steps vary very little from one to another,' Graham explained as they stood at the edge of the floor watching a reel in progress. 'It's the movements which sometimes get complicated. But I'll push you into the right place at the right time, and you'll find the other dancers in the sets only too glad to tell you. It's all good fun and we all help one another.'

Delighted by the brisk regular footwork of the dancers and by the gaiety of the music, Juliet watched entranced, her feet unconsciously trying out the steps. A quick glance at the people present had told her that Lance wasn't there and she knew a sense of relief curiously mixed with disappointment. She hadn't seen him since she had left the car because he hadn't appeared to take dinner with his mother, Jamie and Laura. If he came to the social she had decided not to speak to him, although she found it difficult to subdue the flurry of agitation which she had always felt at the thought of meeting him and which she had once believed to be fear but was now beginning to recognise as excitement.

Soon she was joining the other couples with Graham in a fairly slow dance called a Strathspey to the tune called the *Glasgow Highlanders*. That was followed by *The Gay Gordons*, and by the time that was over her cheeks were glowing and her eyes were sparkling.

The dancing had been so complicated and energetic that she had had no chance to talk to Graham and she realised that any conversation concerning Moira would have to be done between the dances when they either stood or sat at the side of the hall.

She was just about to ask him some leading questions on the subject as they stood getting their breath when Lance spoke behind her.

'You learn quickly, but that was to be expected since your mother was a dancer,' he said.

She stiffened a little but didn't turn to look at him, while the annoyance that she always felt when she learned that he had been watching her unseen flooded through her, making her wary of him. At that moment a resounding chord from the accordion signalled the start of another dance and Graham turned towards her just as Lance slipped an arm about her taut waist.

'My turn, Graham,' he said with his wicked grin. 'You've done your bit for this evening by showing her how.'

Graham's answering smile was indulgent as if he liked the idea of her dancing with Lance although he spoke with pretended disgust.

'Now isn't that just like you, you rogue, sidling up when a fellow isn't looking and taking over his partner. All right, have it your own way. I was thinking I should be asking Laura to dance, anyway. She's looking a wee bit wistful over there because Jamie can't join in. I'll be seeing you Juliet.'

She could have refused to dance with Lance. She could have wrenched out of his hold on her waist and walked away, but she didn't because she knew he would follow her.

151

She knew also that he was careless of the opinion of others and wasn't above making a scene, whereas her shy spirit shied away from drawing attention to herself. No, it would be better to dance one dance with him, not speaking, not even looking at him, which should be easy enough if the dance was another reel or a Strathspey.

But it wasn't either, and as the strains of *Come O'er the Stream, Charlie* started up and he took her right hand in his they moved off into the three-four time of the waltz country dance. He was a good dancer, much better than Graham, who was inclined to be too gangling for co-ordinated movement, and she soon realised that she was enjoying herself. Although it was difficult she managed to keep her head averted, but all the time she was very aware of him watching her.

The dance ended without either of them having spoken, but as they walked to the side of the hall he didn't release her hand, and try as she might she couldn't disengage her fingers from his without the possibility of an undignified scuffle. They were joined by Graham, Laura and Jamie, and some of the other cavers. The conversation was cheerful and general, but there seemed to be no way in which she could approach Graham and speak to him. She hoped he would ask her to dance with him again and that at the end of the dance she would be able to get him by himself, but as the evening wore on her hopes proved fruitless, because he didn't ask her to dance again.

She danced only with Lance, and when they didn't dance but sat watching the others or listening to the singers he was there at her side watching her like an eagle, waiting to swoop as soon as she betrayed herself by moving closer to Graham. And she began to realise, ruefully, when no one else approached her to ask her to dance, that she had been accepted as Lance's partner for the evening as he deliberately cut her off from contact with anyone else.

The hall gradually filled with more people. The dancing grew a little wilder and noisier, and the singing a little sadder. Juliet began to react differently to her unwanted partner. She found she didn't mind any longer if his arm lingered round her waist when they stopped dancing and that she had no desire to avoid looking at him. Indeed the expression in his eyes when they met hers, while they were dancing or talking to the others, was a mixture of challenge and invitation which fascinated her.

After one particularly energetic dance he led her out through the door of the hall to cool off outside. By this time Juliet was under a spell and had forgotten her suspicion that he had been using all his wiles plus a considerable amount of masculine charm to prevent her from talking to Graham. So she went willingly with him down the road, beyond the village lights towards the crumbling walls of a disused wayside chapel.

All around them the rock-bun hills were humped black against the starlit sky and above the distant sugar loaf mountain a crescent moon shone, casting silvery light over the curves and angles of the land. It was a beautiful night, a night for romance, for walking with a lover, thought Juliet dreamily, and she didn't think once of Gareth.

Lance was humming the tune of the last dance as he walked beside her, hands in his pockets, not touching her for the first time since he had appeared by her side in the hall. He stopped humming to tell her that the tune was called *Jock o' Hazeldean* and to ask her if she knew the poem by the same name which had been written by Sir Walter Scott.

'No, I don't. What is it about?' she asked curiously, interested as always in poetry.

'I suppose it's about the triumph of true love over obstacles. In this case the obstacle is a marriage of convenience arranged between the girl in the story and a man called Frank of Errington. But in secret the girl weeps for another young man called Jock of Hazeldean. The wedding is arranged, the groom, the priest and the guests are waiting in the kirk, but the bride never arrives because

"She's o'er the border and awa'
Wi' Jock o' Hazeldean." '

153

He sang the last two lines softly.

'Come to think of it,' he continued, 'Scottish poetry is full of young women ready to defy authority for the sake of love. You'll have heard of Lord Ullin's daughter who preferred "To meet the raging of the skies, But not an angry father" and consequently came to a sad end.'

'It wasn't only the young women who defied authority,' she replied. 'The men did too. Jock of Hazeldean reminds me of one of my favourites, Young Lochinvar, "So faithful in love, and so dauntless in war, There never was knight like the Young Lochinvar!"'

'I might have known he would appeal to you more than Lancelot does,' he remarked dryly, and at once the spell was broken, its gossamer-thin web torn to shreds. Tension was back between them and, upset by the change, Juliet stopped walking and turned to face him. The moonlight tangled in her pale hair and glinted on the granite wall of the old chapel building behind her, as Lance stopped too and looked at her enquiringly.

Wanting to be back within the warmth of the spell, wanting desperately to feel again his arm around her waist and the touch of his hand on hers, Juliet said in a low almost apologetic voice,

'Sir Lancelot only lost his appeal for me when I read of his entanglement with Guinevere, Arthur's wife.'

'You must remember the story was written in the age of chivalry when it was considered the height of romance to love and worship a woman who belonged to another and who was beyond reach,' he replied smoothly, giving nothing away.

'But was she beyond his reach?' she demanded. 'It isn't very clear in the story. In some parts it states that their love was sinful, and then it caused so much trouble, leading Arthur to doubt Lancelot's and Guinevere's loyalty to himself.'

She knew she was treading dangerous ground, but she was daring to do so because she hoped she might prod him into telling her the truth about himself and Moira.

'They both did penance for it later, something of which I'm sure you approve, little puritan,' he replied easily, shrugging off the issue. 'But I'm inclined to agree with you. Lochinvar is much preferable to Lancelot. He knew what he wanted and he went after it.'

He had stepped closer to her and she backed away and was brought up short by the wall of the chapel. The rough granite pricked her hands as she placed them behind her back, the palms flat against the wall to brace herself against his approach.

'What do you want?' she quavered as he stood over her.

'That isn't an easy question to answer,' he murmured. 'Up to this point in my life I've always gone after what I wanted too . . .'

'Regardless of whom you've hurt?' she put in quickly.

'Whom have I hurt?'

'Gareth, perhaps, if you took Moira away from him.'

'So we're back to that! I have to hand it to you, white rose, you don't give up easily, but you'll get no information out of me about Moira—nor out of Graham, for that matter.'

Suspicion was back lying like a sword between them as Juliet realised that while she was out here in the moonlight with him the *ceilidh* would be ending, and Graham would be going back to the cavers' hut and she wouldn't see him to ask the important question: what had Moira done to Gareth? Anger rocketed through her at the thought that Lance had brought her out here deliberately to prevent her from learning more; anger which was spiced by the most agonising disappointment she had ever experienced.

'Oh, don't think I haven't realised that you've done everything you could this evening to keep me from talking to him. You didn't dance with me because you wanted to,' she accused, thinking that if she side-stepped quickly she could dodge him and run up the road to the hall and find Graham before he disappeared into the night.

'Didn't I?' mocked Lance softly, and as if guessing her intention he put both hands against the wall on either side of her, imprisoning her. 'That only goes to show how little you know about me—or even about yourself,' he murmured softly, leaning over her. 'Don't you ever look at yourself, Juliet? If you did you'd see why a man wants to dance with you. Your wide-eyed innocence is a temptation hard to resist. It tempts one to kiss you, to try and wake you up out of your lovely romantic dream where love is cool, remote and chaste, and to show you that it's nothing of the sort.'

She couldn't have moved if she'd tried. Like a small animal hypnotised by the larger one stalking it she shrank back against the wall, knowing he was making love to her and half wishing that he meant what he said. But there was no avoiding him. His hands dropped to her shoulders. He pulled her forward and kissed her ruthlessly on the mouth. For a few seconds her whole body went taut as she tried to reject his embrace, knowing instinctively that it was dangerous to her. Then she felt the warmth of his hands through the thin stuff of her blouse and her resistance to him started to collapse.

With a desperate effort she pulled away from him, raised an arm and swung at his face. As her hand connected, flesh on flesh, he released her suddenly, one of his hands going to his cheek. In that moment she was away, running lightly up the road in the direction of the village. Once she looked back, thinking he might have followed her, wanting to go back and apologise. But the moon-bleached road was empty, and she remembered why he had kissed her and went on.

When she reached the village hall she found the *ceilidh* was over and that people were swarming out into the fine moonlit night, laughing, singing and talking. As she mingled with them she looked for Graham and the other cavers, but there was no sign of them. Her heart still beating crazily from the effect of Lance's kiss, she hurried along to the hotel, thinking that Graham had gone there with Jamie and Laura in the hopes of seeing her.

A light was on in the quiet entrance hall, But there was no one there. She went across to the lounge. Only Laura and Jamie were there, embracing in the dimness. Muttering an apology, Juliet backed out of the room. One hand against her bruised mouth, she began to walk slowly up the stairs, suddenly exhausted by her own emotions, wondering how she was going to explain to Mrs Crimond that she had been unable to find out more about Moira and Gareth from Graham because Lance, with a deliberation which hurt more than anything else he had done or said, had prevented her from doing so, by making love to her.

CHAPTER SIX

Two days later Juliet sat on the terrace at Castle Ross with Gareth. It was past eleven o'clock in the morning and she had been typing for him since eight-thirty, and now they were enjoying the coffee which Vinnie had brought out to them.

It was a fresh sunny morning, and down on the sparkling loch, moving between two dark islands, she could see a white triangle of sail. It was the mainsail of Lance's boat. He had taken Alison sailing with him, and as Juliet watched the blue hull of the boat forging through the water she was shaken by a sudden longing to be aboard, to feel again the spray in her face, to be alone with Lance.

Biting her lip, she looked away from the boat at Gareth. He was lounging in his customary position on the chaise-longue and was looking through a pair of binoculars at the boat. He looked as handsome as ever, and yet she sensed a change in him. She had been noticing it all morning. When he had been dictating to her there had been a new crispness to his pleasant voice and he had moved about much more, pacing slowly up and down the room without his stick. Looking at him now she could also see a different, more determined set to his mouth. There was a brightness, a sharpness about him which had been lacking before. It was as if he had been half asleep during the previous weeks and now he had woken up to reveal his true vitality.

As she watched him, wondering what had brought about the change, he lowered the binoculars and turned to smile at her.

'Alison is at the helm,' he said. 'She'll be enjoying that. She loves to be in control, in the position of command. Do this, Gareth, do that. Ach, she was here on Monday and again on Tuesday, telling me how to exercise my leg.' He gave a self-depreciatory laugh, and added, 'And the annoying thing is I find myself doing what she says when she isn't here.'

'With results,' said Juliet quietly. 'You're walking much better. I believe her intentions are good even if she does seem to be bossy. Like Lance, she would like to see you walking properly again.'

He glanced at her sharply.

'You didn't get lost and you didn't have an accident while you were away, but something happened, because you're not the same,' he accused gently.

'Yes, I am,' she asserted vigorously. In what way had she betrayed herself? When had she revealed that since that moonlit night at Elstone she had changed too? 'I'm still the same silly Juliet with a hopelessly romantic outlook on life. What makes you think I'm different?'

He gazed out at the boat again with a faint puzzled frown between his eyes.

'A feeling, a faint flicker of intuition, call it what you will, that I had when you walked in yesterday afternoon with Lance. You're more wary of him than ever, but you don't hate his guts any more, to use his own inelegant phrase. What happened while you were away?'

She sat very still, aware that his attitude was quite different from the one he had shown on Sunday afternoon when she had returned from Dana Island. This time he wasn't angry, just puzzled and interested.

'Very little,' she replied. 'Graham Lee showed me the Hill of Caves and . . .'

But he didn't allow her to go on.

'Graham Lee?' he interjected. 'His wife was a friend of

158

Moira's at one time. They were students together. Moira used to visit her often when she went over to Edinburgh to shop. Sometimes she'd stay there overnight. But during the past few years she stopped going. I think they may have had a disagreement over something.'

While Juliet was busy digesting this piece of information Vinnie bustled out on to the terrace and whipped the tray from the table, then turned round and snapped,

'Don't think you're going to sit there all day sunning yourself, miss. I could do with Maree taking off my hands. She's a wee divil this morning, in and out of the kitchen stealing my scones and biscuits, upsetting a pint of milk on the floor. Ach, the child's wild about something.'

'I'll come at once,' said Juliet, starting to her feet.

'Wait,' ordered Gareth. 'Vinnie, you have no right to tell Miss Grey what she should be doing. She isn't a kitchen-maid. She wasn't brought here to help you.'

'Humph, I'm often wondering why she was brought here. It wasn't to work, I can tell you that,' snorted the house-keeper, and flounced into the house.

'Lance is back and immediately everyone starts behaving in an irrational manner,' complained Gareth irritably. 'He's to blame for Maree's wildness. She wanted to go with him and Alison this morning and I was willing to let her go because Alison would be there, but he refused to take her. He said he wanted Alison to himself for a few hours and it was impossible while they stayed on land. At her house there's always her mother or her sister or the dogs, and here there's always some sort of interruption. For once I understood how he felt.' He lifted the binoculars to his eyes and looked down the loch again to the distant boat.

'I wonder if he'll manage to find some way of keeping Alison out all night too,' he murmured more to himself than to her.

Juliet recognised the new shock which ripped through her as jealousy, nothing else—jealousy because Alison was alone with Lance on the boat and might not return to-night. Once again she sprang to her feet.

'I'll go and find Maree,' she muttered.

But he didn't seem to hear her, being more intent on watching the boat, and as she went through the lounge she couldn't help thinking that before she had gone to Elstone he would not have let her leave the terrace so easily but would have found some reason for her to stay with him until lunchtime.

Maree was only too glad to help pack a picnic lunch and to take Juliet on a fishing expedition to the Black Pool. Having learned how the tie flies and to cast from McVinn she was delighted to have an opportunity to show off her knowledge to a complete novice like Juliet, and she carried the fishing rods and the box containing the flies willingly while Juliet carried the lunch in a small canvas haversack slung over her shoulder.

'Aunty Alison likes fishing too,' she said, as they walked through the woodland on the lower slopes of the hill at the back of the castle. 'She says Uncle Lance taught her how to tie flies and how to cast when they were younger. I hope he marries her and then she'll be my real aunt. We had great fun with her while you were away. Even Daddy was more fun. She makes him walk without his stick. She doesn't care what she says to him. At first he roared back at her, but then he began to laugh and we all laughed together. Do you think Uncle Lance will marry her?'

He's probably working on that just now, thought Juliet waspishly, but aloud she said only,

'I know very little about them, Maree, and it isn't really any of my business. I'm only an employee like Vinnie.'

Maree grimaced with disgust.

'That sounds horrid,' she complained. 'I don't think of either of you like that, and Vinnie isn't an employee, she's one of the family. She used to look after Daddy and Uncle Lance and Uncle Jamie when they were boys. She told me she's been more of a mother to them than a grannie, especially when they stayed here. She used to make them wash behind their ears, and change their wet clothes so that they wouldn't catch cold, and give them the right sort of food.'

'But your grannie looked after them when they were in Glasgow.'

'No, she didn't, because they went away to boarding school in Edinburgh. I'm going to boarding school next month.' A fierce rebellious expression darkened Maree's face. 'I don't want to go. I want to stay here with Daddy and Vinnie and you and Aunty Alison.'

'If your Aunty Alison marries your uncle she won't be here, because he doesn't live here all the time,' said Juliet absently, wondering why the thought of Lance marrying Alison made her feel so wretched.

'I suppose not,' sighed Maree regretfully, then with a quick change of mood, her face lighting up with a new idea, she added, 'Perhaps Daddy could marry her. They seem to like each other quite well even though they argue a lot.' Another black frown chased away the light from her face. 'But I suppose Uncle Lance wouldn't like that. Oh dear, grown-ups are so funny. They never seem to see things straight. Everyone says I need a mother to look after me, and Aunty Alison would suit me fine. Here we are at last. Isn't it a perfect spot for fishing? I hope you've made plenty of sandwiches, because I'm awfully hungry.'

There was no doubt that the Black Pool was a beautiful place to spend an afternoon. It was about forty yards in width, very deep and dark under bluffs of rock on one side but shallowing steadily to the middle where a ridge of rock stood well out of the water. On the near side it was no deeper than a foot or two and it shallowed to a few inches bordering the gravelly spit on which they stood.

On the steep slopes opposite there were larch and pine trees, a pattern of light and dark green, while over all arched the blue sky, specked with little puffs of white cloud. The whole place was full of warm, lazy, dappled light and Juliet felt remote and safe there in the wide hollow of the hills, as she concentrated on learning how to tie a fly correctly and how to cast it, so that it lay on top of the water, a small delicate smudge of colour to tantalise the fish lurking in the shadowy depths of the pool.

161

The afternoon passed pleasantly and she forgot for a while the thoughts which had been tormenting her ever since she had left Lance by the old chapel in the moonlight, and it was not until she and Maree were returning downhill to the castle and she caught sight of the blue boat running up the loch under full sail, its striped spinnaker billowing out in front, that the turmoil started up again.

While she washed and changed for dinner she took herself to task. Why should she feel jealous of Alison Coates? Why should she be suffering this deep-seated envy? It wasn't as if she were in love with Lance any more than she was in love with Gareth.

Not in love with Gareth! Juliet sank down on the edge of her bed and stared at the sea-green ribbon which she held in her hand and which she was going to use to tie her hair back. It matched exactly the colour of the dress she had worn at Hilary's wedding and which she had decided to wear in an effort to boost her spirits.

But now this strange thought coming out of the chaos of her mind made her pause. She wasn't in love with Gareth! For a while she had been infatuated with him, a quite natural development for someone as lonely as herself on meeting someone as charming and as handsome as he was. It had been a feeling similar to a schoolgirl crush. To her romantic mind he had represented a stricken knight, straight out of a fairy tale, who had required help and comfort, and she had been ready to give him both.

But the infatuation had died while she had been away at Elstone and she suspected it had begun to fade earlier, possibly in a cave on an island. She didn't love him and even if he asked her, as Mrs Crimond and Lance both hoped he would, she couldn't marry him. She couldn't marry him because she couldn't bear to have Lance as her brother-in-law.

She made a little sound of distress and going hurriedly to the mirror she tied up her hair and fled from the bedroom down the wheel stair, her long skirt billowing out behind her, through the joining passage into the lounge, where the

162

sound of laughter greeted her and she was no longer alone.

Everyone was in the lounge. Alison was there, her red head like a flaming torch against Lance's dark sweater as she laughed up at him. Laura and Jamie were there, trying to sit together in one armchair. Gareth was there, lounging on the settee, his eyes bright as he looked at Alison and Lance. Mrs Crimond was there smiling happily, enjoying the unusual moment of harmony in her family and Maree was there, hair brushed, face scrubbed, linking her arm affectionately through Alison's.

It was a family gathering and for a moment Juliet, hovering inside the door, felt forlorn, left out. She didn't belong, and she wasn't needed now that they had Alison.

Then across the red hair Lance's eyes met hers. His cool glance swept over the sea-green dress and then back to her troubled face. He moved away from Alison and came across to her.

'The return of the white rose,' he murmured. 'I wondered where you'd gone. Come and join us. We're having a premature celebration of Laura and Jamie's engagement.'

She ignored the hand he held out to her and walked past him, her face pale and taut, her head held high.

'Yes, come and have a drink,' said Jamie, struggling out of the chair in which he seemed to have been tightly wedged beside Laura.

'Champagne, of course. Lance said nothing else would do for a celebration of this sort. I hope you like it.'

'Yes, she likes it, don't you, Juliet?'

Lance was beside her again, taking the glass which Jamie had filled and handing it to her. When he had welcomed her into the room it had been the first time he had spoken to her since she had slapped his face and she found herself wondering suspiciously what lay behind his unexpectedly friendly approach. She made no effort to respond and didn't look at him as she took the proffered glass and murmured her thanks.

'Now that we're all here,' said Mrs Crimond, smiling warmly at Juliet and immediately dispelling that feeling of loneliness which had attacked Juliet on entering the room, 'I should like to make another toast. First to Laura and Jamie, wishing them every happiness for the future, then to Alison and Lance, hoping they will soon follow the good example set by these two young people, and then to Juliet and Gareth, hoping that the hard work which they are doing together in the mornings will result in a more lasting relationship.'

Everyone laughed, raised their glasses and then sipped their drinks. Alison turned and smiled at Lance, then her glance drifted slowly to Juliet, who was still standing beside him. The smile still lingering on her mouth, she came across and deliberately stood between them as if to make sure they wouldn't talk to each other, while Jamie chaffed his mother affectionately for trying to push people around as she did the characters in her books.

'But I don't push them around,' complained Mrs Crimond. 'They act of their own accord, but occasionally I have to restrain them and point out the way they should be taking.'

'Which is what you've just been doing to all of us,' he mocked, and immediately a lively argument started between the two of them.

'Maree tells me you've been fishing the Black Pool this afternoon,' said Alison to Juliet, 'and that you caught your first fish.'

'Beginners' luck,' taunted Lance, and Alison turned to him.

'I seem to remember you teasing me in just the same way years ago. Why don't we go there to-morrow?'

'Maybe we will, but I'm not promising anything,' he replied easily.

'Lance wasn't the only one you used to fish that pool with,' put in Gareth, limping up to them. He was without his stick and stood tall, taller than his brother, more handsome in his more colourful slightly flamboyant clothes, looking down at Alison as if they shared a secret. 'Do you

164

remember when you fell in the pool and I had to rescue you?'

'I remember,' replied Alison, turning to smile at him, and it seemed to Juliet, who was suddenly aware of undercurrents of feeling, that the smile was warmer, more spontaneous when bestowed on Gareth, as Alison remembered another incident which had involved him years ago when they had spent their holidays together.

And all through dinner it was like that, Gareth at his best, his eyes vivid in his thin face as he recalled one escapade after another in which he and Alison, or he and Lance, or all three of them had participated when young. It was inevitable that with his gift for story-telling and mimicry he should outshine his eldest brother, and he was really very attractive and very lovable, thought Juliet after laughing at one of the more amusing anecdotes, and one couldn't really blame Alison for giving him all her attention, turning away from Lance on whose left she was sitting.

But as Juliet watched Gareth and Alison share laughter from her own position across the table on Lance's right she became aware of Lance's silence. Normally she wouldn't have thought it unusual for him to be quiet because he rarely talked at the table, but to-night he had at first been more expansive than she had ever known him, so that now his withdrawal from the conversation was more noticeable.

She glanced sideways at him. He didn't seem to be paying much attention to the others at all and looked as if his thoughts were far away and judging by the frown which darkened his face they weren't very pleasant.

A cold chill swept over Juliet. It must have been like this when he had brought Moira home, she thought. He must have sat silently watching and hearing Gareth charm her and win her away from him ... and she wondered whether the same situation could repeat itself in the same family. Was it possible that the two brothers were destined to fall in love again with the same woman? With Alison?

There must be something she could do to prevent Alison

from hurting Lance as Moira had once hurt him. Perhaps if she made an effort she could draw Gareth's attention away from the lovely vivacious redhead. After all, even if she wasn't in love with him, Gareth had seemed attracted to herself. Acting impulsively she leaned forward across the table and spoke to Gareth, just as Lance roused himself and spoke to Alison, and from then on Juliet managed to hold Gareth's attention until the meal finished.

He walked with her to the lounge from the dining-room leaving Alison to come with Lance, and Juliet felt a bitter-sweet satisfaction in knowing that she had helped Lance indirectly. But when Alison eventually stepped out on to the terrace to join the rest of them, she was alone. She informed them that Lance had been called to the telephone and would come later, but as the evening wore on he never came, and when Maree persuaded Alison to play the piano to her before she went to bed and they both went into the lounge, Gareth followed them.

Juliet knew that she should follow him, but since Jamie and Laura had also left the terrace to go for a walk her good manners wouldn't allow her to leave Mrs Crimond alone. So she sat on watching the gloaming deepen to night, seeing the stars come out one by one to glitter in the dark blue velvet of the sky, listening with only half an ear to Mrs Crimond's plans for the party she intended to hold at the week-end when Laura's parents would come to stay at the castle.

After a while she realised that the piano music had stopped. She guessed that Maree had gone to bed, and wondered why Gareth and Alison had not returned to the terrace. Mrs Crimond rose to her feet.

'We've had a very pleasant evening, one of the best I've known for some time. I wonder where Lance is? It's time he took Alison home. Just peep into the lounge, will you, dear, and see if he's there with her and Gareth.'

When Juliet looked into the room she found it dim and empty. Only one lamp was lit close to the piano.

'There's no one there,' she reported back to Mrs Crimond.

'Then Lance has taken her home. Strange that she didn't come to say good-night. Alison is usually so particular about little things like that, but perhaps he hurried her. Well, I suppose we may as well go to bed. Gareth must have gone already. I think he enjoyed this evening too. It's a long time since I've seen him so lively. There's been such an improvement in him during the last few weeks, which only goes to prove that time is a healer—although I also think I have you to thank, my dear.' She patted Juliet's cheek in an affectionate manner. 'I'll just take a walk round the garden before going up. It's another beautiful night. The weather has really been remarkable for the last day or so.'

She went off down the steps, and Juliet, feeling curiously flat as if she had just witnessed a play to which there had been no climax, went up to her room. Sleepy after her afternoon with the fish, she prepared quickly for bed, sure that she would fall asleep straight away. But once she had lain down all the evening's events paraded before her and she could not sleep.

She kept thinking about Gareth and his deliberate attempt to monopolise Alison's attention. He had revealed himself to be quite as capable of tormenting others as Lance was. For once their positions had been reversed.

But had Lance been tormented? She hoped not. It was possible that he was too sure of Alison to be worried, and if Mrs Crimond's assessment of Alison's feelings was correct there was no fear of Lance losing her to Gareth as he had lost Moira. Yet according to Graham Lee Lance had ended up disliking Moira for what she had done to Gareth.

Juliet twisted restlessly. What was the use of her lying here racking her brains trying to solve a mystery which Lance had no intention of allowing her to solve? And why did it matter so much to her? It would be better if she followed Mrs Crimond's advice given the other night in the hotel bedroom at Elstone after she had explained she had

167

been unable to extract any more information from Graham about Moira. The older woman had sighed a little and then had said,

'If Lance thinks you shouldn't know, then leave it that way. He's often very wise about this sort of thing, so please forget I asked you to find out.'

Juliet turned again in bed. Since she couldn't sleep she might as well read. Reading would prevent her from tossing and turning and would perhaps provide her with a new mystery which she would be free to solve.

She swung out of bed, found her dressing gown and pulled it on, and crept barefoot into the passage. The light was still on. Had Lance forgotten to put it off on his way to bed, or was he still with Alison? She dragged her thoughts away from that disturbing direction and flitted silently down the wheel stair.

Lights were also burning in the passageway and in the lounge the light beside the piano was still on. Going straight to the bookcase, she searched the shelves for something which might appeal and eventually chose a light mystery novel.

On her way out of the room she paused to turn off the lamp by the piano and noticed that the curtains at the French window were swaying slightly. The window was still open. Wondering a little at Vinnie's unusual carelessness, to which the burning lights and the open window were witness, she went to close the window.

Outside she could see moonlight reflected on the still water of the loch and tempted by the serenity of the scene she stepped out on to the terrace. Crossing over to the balustrade, she leaned there for a moment, fascinated by the dazzling glitter of silver on the water.

The familiar creak of the springs of the chaise-longue, the sound of something being set down on the side table brought her whirling round hand to mouth to stifle a spontaneous cry of alarm.

'Gareth?' she queried nervously.

'Sorry to disappoint you,' Lance's voice was lazily sardonic. 'Were you expecting to find him here?'

'No, I . . .' she began, and had to stop because the pounding of her heart made speech difficult. Whenever would she get used to finding him where she least expected him to be? 'What are you doing here?' she managed to say at last.

'Sitting thinking,' he answered carelessly. As she approached the chaise-longue she noticed moonlight reflecting on the glass he had just set down on the table, the glint of his light eyes in his shadowed face as he looked up at her, even the lock of dark hair which had slipped forward. He had been lying on the chaise-longue, but as she came near he rose to his feet automatically with those impeccable good manners which either Mrs Crimond or Vinnie had drummed into all three Crimond brothers.

'Why are you flitting about the house, half-dressed, when you should be in bed?' he asked.

'I'm not half-dressed,' she retorted defensively, curving her arms around her waist to hold her dressing gown closer to her body.

'I think you are,' he drawled, and she was suddenly glad there wasn't much light on the terrace. 'You must be finding it chilly out here in your bare feet. Do you often wander through the house at night?'

'No, of course not,' she snapped, wishing she hadn't seen the open window and hadn't been tempted to step out on to the terrace.

'Then if you haven't a secret assignation with Gareth and you're not walking in your sleep, what are you doing here? I won't flatter myself by thinking you've come down in the hopes of meeting me.'

There was an insolent kick to all his comments which roused her temper

'I don't make assignations,' she replied haughtily. 'I came to get a book to read because I couldn't sleep. I noticed the window was open, so I came to close it and was tempted to come out on the terrace to see the moonlight on the water.'

'Another night for lovers, but a little wasted on you and

me, don't you think? You don't like being kissed by me and I don't like having my face slapped,' he remarked acidly, and her cheeks flamed at his reference to the last time they had been alone together in the moonlight. 'So you couldn't sleep,' he continued. 'Because Gareth seemed to prefer Alison's charms to yours this evening, perhaps?'

What a foul mood he was in! She couldn't let him get away with a sneer like that even though she wanted to turn and run from his scorn.

'Perhaps it's because she seemed to prefer his charms to yours that you're here, sitting thinking,' her glance went deliberately to the empty glass, and she added in mimicry of his own acidity, 'and drinking.'

But as usual he seemed to find her attempt to taunt him amusing. He put his head back and laughed making her want to slap him again.

'Well done,' he mocked. 'But you're wrong. My reason for sitting out here and thinking and drinking is not as romantic as you would like to think. Like you I was tempted out by the moonlight to enjoy an hour or so of peace. Unfortunately to-night business reared its ugly head and to-morrow I have to return to work. There are contracts to be signed and appointments to be kept.'

'And money to be made,' she put in tartly, and he laughed again.

'That too,' he agreed, then added almost wistfully, 'And just now I don't want to leave Castle Ross.'

He didn't want to go because of Alison, she thought, but her own first reaction to the news that he was going away was one of immense relief. She would be free at last from the eagle gaze, and the castle would return to normal, become once again the oasis of peaceful gracious living which she had known before he had arrived.

But hard on the heels of that first reaction came another. He was going and she might never see him again.

'Do I sense a feeling of relief on your part?' he jibed. 'Perhaps I ought to warn you that I'll be back later in September to take the boat round to the Clyde to have it

170

hauled out for the winter.'

'I shall be gone before then,' Juliet replied, surprising herself as well as him. She wasn't sure when she had come to the decision that she must leave or why she had made it.

'Am I to regard that as formal notice of leaving your position as Tess's secretary?' he asked coldly.

'Yes, I think so,' she replied uncertainly.

'You think so? You're not sure? Does that mean you spoke on the spur of the moment, acting on a silly impulse? You'd better be sure, Juliet, because I've no time for ditherers,' he snapped.

'Oh, yes, I'd forgotten you're cold-blooded and business-like and rarely give in to impulse youself, so how can I expect you to understand?' she retorted. 'Yes, I intend to leave.'

'May I ask why?' He was scrupulously polite suddenly, having withdrawn behind that icy film.

Desperately she searched for a reason which would not betray her real feelings, about which she was in a state of confusion anyway.

'I don't get on with Vinnie,' she said vaguely.

'You don't . . .?' he began incredulously. 'Good God, do you really expect me to swallow that excuse?' he exclaimed, politeness cast aside. 'Everyone gets on with Vinnie.'

'Well, I don't—at least she doesn't get on with me. She dislikes me for some reason, and goes out of her way to make me feel unwanted and unnecessary here. Only this morning she said she couldn't understand why I'm employed here. There are times when I don't understand either. Actually there's very little for me to do and . . .'

'If Vinnie's attitude is all that's upsetting you,' he interrupted coldly, cutting across her tumbling words, 'I'll speak to her and get her off your back.'

'Oh, no!' She was dismayed now and feeling a little shaky. She hadn't bargained for this sort of confrontation wih him at this hour of the night, or rather the early morning, and was beginning to wish she had turned right round and left the terrace when she had discovered he was there. 'Please don't take her to task. She resents it terribly when you do, although she says she doesn't. But I know she does because the whole household suffers as a result.'

'Does it, indeed?' he commented dryly. 'Then it will have to suffer, because I'm not having her thinking she can say what she likes to you, and I can't understand why she thinks you're not needed. Mother needs you, and Maree . . .'

'Maree has Alison now, and will be going to school soon. She doesn't need me.'

He was silent for a second or two, looking down at her, trying to read the expression on her face which was bleached by moonlight.

'Gareth needs you,' he suggested quietly.

'I doubt it. Alison has done more for him than I have. She has made him walk.'

Again he was silent. Then turning away he walked over to the balustrade and stood looking out over the loch.

'You said the other day that the decision to leave or to stay was mine,' she said, in a small voice, aware that her last remark concerning Alison had gone home and had hurt him in some way.

He turned and leaned on the balustrade, his face in the shadow now and unreadable.

'That was because I was angry with you for probing,' he replied flatly. 'The decision still rests with you and always will, Juliet, but I think you would be very foolish to allow your jealousy of Alison to drive you away from here.'

She should have been used to his ability to put his finger on the hub of her thoughts by now, but she wasn't, and her outraged gasp betrayed her. He pushed away from the balustrade and came close to her, his bulk blotting out the radiance of the moon, casting a shadow over her.

'There's no need for you to be jealous of Alison,' he said swiftly, confidently. 'That little performance put on by Gareth last evening was directed more at me than at you. He was getting his own back for Saturday night. He even went so far as to take her home.'

'But how? He told me he couldn't drive, that his leg . . .' She stopped, bewildered.

'As I've always thought, Gareth's leg isn't paralysed. He only convinced himself that it was and stopped using it, and indirectly you have helped him to use it. He was so wildly jealous because I kept you out all night on Saturday, quite unintentionally as it happened, and because you went with me to Elstone, that he forced himself to do things he hasn't done for almost three years, in order to get back at me.'

'By making you jealous?'

'Exactly. You see there's always been a certain amount of natural jealousy between us, as well as some very healthy rivalry. When we were boys he always wanted what I had and when we grew older it began to apply to girls. I brought them home and he took them over. I think I've told you what a bad effect his accident plus Moira's death had on him. He became so unlike himself, so lethargic and self-pitying, I had to try and do something about it. But nothing I did seemed to have any effect, not even deliberately taunting him.'

He paused and drew a deep breath, and she had the impression that having to explain to her was a chore he disliked heartily.

'When I came here to collect Mother to take her to London a few months ago I was so disgusted with him that I lost my temper. Mother had suggested he should marry again and he was moaning that no woman these days would settle for a crippled husband who already had a wilful, wayward child, and I blew my top and told him that I'd find him another wife just as I'd found the last. It wasn't a very nice thing to say, but it got results. For the first time for years he seemed to be himself and he bet me I couldn't find anyone suitable, and it occurred to me that perhaps the one way I could shake him out of his miserable lethargy was to accept the bet and to bring home a girl.'

'Me,' whispered Juliet.

'Yes, you. The very fact that I'd found you made him

interested in you from the start.'

'But why me?'

'I must confess that by the time I attended that wedding I was beginning to think that I'd never find anyone suitable. Then I saw you and you looked right. I talked to you and found you were innocent and idealistic, ridiculously romantic in your attitude to marriage, and that seemed right too. I discovered you were out of work and that you were Norma Thomas's daughter. The rest I left to Mother.'

Lance will do anything for the members of his family. Graham's remark came back to her. That anything had inluded selecting her as a suitable second wife for Gareth, persuading his mother to choose her as her secretary so that she could be brought to Castle Ross, and then depending on his brother's charm to do the rest. And it had succeeded, or almost.

'I suppose you think you've won the bet?' she challenged in a low furious voice.

'Not yet. I win only when he asks you to marry him and you accept.'

'You're very sure of that happening,' she seethed. 'You can't make me stay and do that.'

'No. I can only rely on my first impression of you. I thought then you had certain qualities, tenderness and a strong sense of loyalty, which would help you to stay the course. Now that I've told you that your reasons for leaving aren't very sound because Vinnie can be dealt with and Alison presents no real threat, I don't think you'll want to leave.'

He thought he had trapped her, that he was, as always, right, but there was something over which he had no control.

'You've forgotten something in your calculations,' she said on a note of triumph. 'People don't fall in love to order just to help others to win bets.'

'I'm well aware of that, but what has it to do with you and Gareth?'

'I'm not in love with him,' she asserted firmly.

174

'Oh. Are you sure?' he drawled softly. 'Then why are you jealous of Alison?'

The book slipped from her nerveless fingers. Suddenly she was without protection, exposed and vulnerable to his mockery. He bent and picked the book up and held it out.

'Go to bed, Juliet,' he ordered quietly, almost kindly, with that sort of indulgent kindness one expected from fathers or grandfathers or uncles, making her want to stamp her feet and scream at him that she preferred his taunts. 'None of us are at our best in the small hours of the morning. You'll see everything differently when you've slept. Goodbye for now. I'll expect to see you here when I come again in September.'

She took the book from him and fled.

CHAPTER SEVEN

THE engagement party held for Laura and Jamie the following week-end was a great success. Mr and Mrs Penny, being slightly overawed by the castle and by Mrs Crimond, had no objections to their daughter becoming engaged to Jamie as long as the couple didn't marry until Laura had attained her eighteenth birthday. They took both Laura and Jamie back with them to Edinburgh, where Jamie hoped to get better treatment for the cracked bone in his arm.

With their departure coming so closely after Lance's silent and almost unnoticed exit, Juliet fully expected the way of life at the castle to return to the same leisurely pace which she had known before Lance had arrived, and to a certain extent it did. Vinnie was pleasant and smiling again and not once did she give Juliet a disapproving glance or make any harsh remarks about her employment there. Mrs Crimond's story progressed in leaps and bounds so that she typed every afternoon, and Gareth had truly come to life. With the returning use of his leg he was walking more and more without his stick and becoming more independent, often going off by himself somewhere in the estate car. He spent less time lounging on the terrace and actually talked of leaving the castle once Maree had gone to her boarding school in Edinburgh.

This last suggestion which he made one evening at dinner startled his mother.

'But what will you do? Where will you go?' she asked rather querulously.

'I shall go to Edinburgh too. I shall rent a flat there,' he replied confidently.

'All the teaching positions at the University will be filled now,' said Mrs Crimond, a little tremulously. 'What will you do for a living?'

'Write,' was the succinct reply.

'But you can write here. You are writing here.'

'Not as well as I would if I were on my own. To do what I want to do I have to have access to records, government reports, museums. I can live on my allowance out of Father's estate as long as Lance doesn't mind footing the bill for Maree's education for a while, until I start earning again.'

The change in him was for the better, Juliet could see that now, and she began to understand why Lance had done what he had done, and with understanding came forgiveness. His intention had been good even if his way of achieving it had been a little strange. But as the days went by she realised that there was no chance of him winning his bet with Gareth because it was quite obvious to her that there was no room for her, or any other woman, as far as she could tell, in Gareth's plans for his future. In a way she was relieved because it meant that he wasn't in love with her any more than she was with him, so that there was no possibility of him asking her to marry him, much to Mrs Crimond's disappointment.

'At one point I really thought you and he might make a go of it,' she said. 'So much for wishful thinking. I've always been guilty of it. I hope your feelings aren't hurt,

176

Juliet.'

'Oh, no. I think we were both attracted to each other at first. I'd never met anyone like him before and he went to my head a little.'

'Mm, I understand, and I think you went to his, because for so long he'd cut himself off from the society of pretty young women. I'm glad you're not hurt, although there is something wrong, isn't there?'

'What do you mean?' asked Juliet warily.

'You're not quite the same as you were when I first met you. You're not untouched by the more violent emotions, not so innocent. You look as if someone has woken you up rather rudely.'

At that moment the telephone rang. The caller asked for Mrs Crimond and Juliet was able to escape upstairs to her bedroom. For all that she seemed so vague Mrs Crimond noticed far too much, she thought, as she peered out of her window. The weather was heavy and humid. Beneath low cloud the loch lay sullenly smooth, pewter-coloured. Already it was mid-September and in the few scattered fields the oats and barley had been harvested and stooked. To-morrow Maree would be leaving for her hated boarding school and Gareth would be going to his flat in Edinburgh and she would be left with Mrs Crimond to wait for the arrival of Lance.

She must leave before he came, but how? Acting on sudden impulse she left her room and went down to the lounge where she was sure she had seen a local bus time-table. If she could persuade McVinn to take her into Lochmoyhead without saying anything to anyone, she could catch a bus from there to Adrishaig and from there she could go on to Tarbert and get a ferry to Gourock, thence by train to Glasgow, and on to London.

It was while she was leafing through the time-table that she heard the sound of voices raised angrily, followed by the slamming of a door. One voice she recognised as Gareth's in one of his thunder-and-lightning moods, but the other hadn't sounded like Maree's, more like Alison's.

Juliet frowned as she traced with her finger the times of buses leaving Lochmoyhead. They weren't very frequent. One every other day, in fact.

Hearing a sound, she looked up. Alison had come into the lounge and not noticing her had sunk down on the arm of a chair. She was blowing her nose and the tears were streaming down her face. Sympathy, a quality of which Juliet had a superabundance, surged up and flinging down the time-table she went across to the weeping woman.

'Alison, what's wrong? Is there anything I can do to help?'

Alison spun round. Her topaz eyes blazed through her tears.

'Oh, it's you! Yes, you can help—by going away, far away, back to where you came from before Lance picked you up. He has a tendency to pick up stray cats, you know, because he's sorry for them and wants to give them a home.'

Although Juliet stiffened all over in reaction to the insult which had just been hurled at her she was determined to keep her cool, realising that Alison was very upset.

'Why do you want me to go?' she asked mildly. 'What have I done to harm you?'

'You've taken Gareth away from me,' wailed Alison, 'just as Moira did.'

'But ... but I thought you were in love with Lance and going to marry him.'

'Me in love with that iceberg? No, never. Oh, I like Lance well enough, but I've always loved Gareth and we might have married if Lance hadn't brought Moira home just as he brought you, and I hoped when I heard that she'd died that there was a chance he might ...' Alison started to sob noisily and Juliet had to wait for the sobs to subside before she could make herself heard.

'Gareth doesn't love me,' she said quietly, when Alison had stopped crying and was just sniffing.

'But you're going with him to Edinburgh,' said Alison, her eyes wide.

'No. I'm staying here with Mrs Crimond. I'm employed to work for her, you know.'

'Yes, I know,' muttered Alison, pulling at her handkerchief nervously, then with a fresh burst of tears she cried out, 'Oh, what have I done, what have I done?'

'Alison, please, you'll make yourself ill,' pleaded Juliet, who was really perturbed by the other woman's anguish. 'You'd better tell me what you've done.'

'I told him about Moira. I told him how she cheated and lied to him, how she used to say she'd gone to stay with friends when all the time she was with other men. I told him that it was her fault his leg didn't get better because it suited her to have him immobile while she could go and enjoy herself. I told him that she wasn't with Lance that time she was stuck for three days in the Cairngorms, nor was she with him when she was killed. He used to let her go when she said she was going with Lance, because he trusted Lance, and all those years he trusted her and she ended by destroying his trust in his brother.'

'But how did you know all this.' asked Juliet.

'I knew because Helen Lee told me when I met her recently. When I met Lance he told me I wasn't to say anything to Gareth about it because Gareth still thought Moira was perfect and that it would break his heart to learn differently.'

'Then why did you tell him now?'

'Oh, because he's going away, because he wouldn't take any notice of me, and because I thought I was afraid the same thing was going to happen all over again with you in Moira's place, because I know you don't love Gareth. It's Lance who fascinates you, isn't it? But like Moira you'd marry second best just to get a comfortable home.'

'Alison, stop it. Please!'

Alison sniffed, looked up into Juliet's troubled eyes and apologised,

'I'm sorry, I shouldn't have said that. I'm in such a state I don't know what I'm saying any more. Oh, my poor

Gareth! His face when I told him. What am I going to do?'

'You're going back to him and you're going to apologise to him as you've just apologised to me,' said Juliet firmly. 'Tell him your own strong feelings for him carried you away, made you say unkind things. Tell him you love him, but for goodness' sake go back to him now.'

'Excuse me, miss,' Vinnie spoke from the doorway, and it was quite obvious from the gleam in her black eyes that she had heard every word Juliet had just said, 'have you seen Maree? It's getting late and there's a heavy mist on the hills. It's time she was in and packing her clothes ready for to-morrow.'

'No, I haven't seen her. Have you, Alison?'

'She was with Gareth and me. We were talking about her going to school, and she suddenly jumped up and ran out of the room.'

'That'll be the root of it, I shouldn't wonder,' sighed Vinnie, and her plump face looked aged with worry. 'She's run off because she doesn't want to go. Ach, I'm getting old and I can't be doing with tantrums and wilfulness any more. Would you mind going and looking for her, miss? McVinn is away to Tarbert all day or I'd be asking him. If she gets lost in the mist Mr Gareth and Mr Lance will never forgive me.'

'Mr Gareth should be going to look for his own child,' said Alison, rising to her feet. 'I'll go and tell him.'

'I've been already, but he's not in a good mood. Ach, it's one of those days when a body can't be saying or doing the right thing.'

'It's all right, Vinnie, I'll go,' comforted Juliet. 'I'll find her. She won't be far away.'

'That's good of you, miss. There was a time when I was thinking you were another come to wreck yon man's peace of mind like the other one did, but now I know I was wrong.' Then turning to Alison she said, 'Aye, lass, you go along to him and tell him. He needs someone like you, Miss Alison.'

As the housekeeper left the room muttering to herself Alison and Juliet stared at one another.

'Perhaps I'd better come with you to look for Maree,' began Alison uncertainly.

'No, you go to Gareth. Only you can put it right. Don't you see, Alison?'

'I hope you're right. I do hope you're right. But be careful on the hills. Don't get lost. Maree knows her way blindfolded by now, I should think, but you don't. Make for the Black Pool. That's her favourite place, as it used to be for all of us when we were in trouble or unhappy.'

Juliet remembered Alison's warning later when, blindfolded by the thick clinging mist, unable to see her way and unsure of her whereabouts, she stood ankle-deep in bog myrtle and admitted to herself that she was lost.

When she had left the castle she had taken Alison's advice and had started off towards the Black Pool. At first she had had no trouble as only an occasional wreath of mist had twisted across the path as she had climbed higher and higher, keeping the sound of the tumbling river to her left. Every so often she had called Maree's name and had waited for an answer, until the thought had occurred to her that if Maree didn't want to be found she wouldn't answer.

What was the use of searching for the girl if she didn't want to be found? With her knowledge of the area Maree would have many hiding places where she could stay until hunger drove her down to the castle. Or was it possible that she had run away properly, walking to Lochmoyhead and taking the bus or hitching a lift somewhere, anywhere as long as she didn't have to go to the school in Edinburgh?

It was while she had been thinking that the mist had come down in earnest and she had decided then she had better go back to the castle, when she discovered that she had no idea which way she should go. She had thought she could hear the river's song to her left, and that if she walked towards the sound she could keep close to it, walk downhill and eventually come out on the road leading from

Lochmoyhead to the castle. But she hadn't found the river again, so she had begun to walk downhill anyway, and as she had walked the stories which Gareth had told her about people being lost for whole days and nights on the hills and of some who had never been found because they had walked into bogs came to haunt her. For a while she had been unable to go any farther, thinking that if she did she might step into one of those deceitful patches of green and become its captive.

A little later the mist had lifted helpfully and she had caught sight of the old bothy which she recognised from the time she had gone fishing with Maree. The sight of it cheered her and, glad to have some sort of bearings at last, she had started down the hill again.

But the mist had come back obliterating everything. She had trudged on doggedly, tumbling over unseen tussocks of grass, turning her ankle painfully on a hidden rock. Her hair clung to her head damply and the lower part of her legs and her feet were soaking wet.

It was when she had heard, or had thought she had heard, a voice calling her name that she had stopped again. Had she heard it or was it her imagination playing tricks? Once more Gareth's stories crowded into her mind and she had recalled his advice not to move if the mist came down but to sit and wait. If something called to her she wasn't to move but was to stay still, for if she wandered in the mist, the mist would hang about her and she would never find her way. Never, never was she to obey voices that she heard calling.

So she had taken that remembered advice and had stayed put in the middle of a moor and had admitted she was lost.

Soon she began to shiver. If only, she thought, she had stopped when she had seen the bothy. And quite suddenly, as if in answer to her thought, the mist lifted uncannily and she saw the sky pricked with stars and the dark angular outline of the bothy ahead.

She didn't stop to wonder why it was in front of her and

not behind her but hurried towards it while she could see it, hobbling a little because she had developed a blister on the back of one of her heels.

Reaching the door, she groped her way into the lime-washed building, which consisted of a single room. When her eyes had become accustomed to the gloom she found that it was furnished by a table and two chairs and sitting down thankfully on one of the chairs she decided to stay there and wait.

By now everyone at Castle Ross must be wondering where she was and why she hadn't returned with Maree. Would Gareth organise a search party to look for them? Or would he be too unhappy, too sunk in misery to spare a thought for either her or his daughter? Not if Alison had been successful he wouldn't. How silly of her not to have noticed that Alison was in love with Gareth. Did Lance know she was, or was it a shock in store for him?

The intrusion of Lance into her thoughts set her moving. She had discovered during the past weeks that the only way to avoid thinking about him was to do something, anything. Now she hobbled to the door and looked out. The mist was back, blotting out the starry sky, reducing visibility to nothing.

Juliet hobbled back to her chair and had hardly sat down when she thought she heard her name being called. It must be the voice of the mist calling her again. She wouldn't go to the door again. She wouldn't go out, because if she did she would get lost.

There are more ways of getting lost than falling down a pothole. Graham had said that. He had also said that if she had been his property he wouldn't have let her go roaming the countryside with Lance. She knew now what he had meant. She had gone to Dana with Lance, had gone to the caves with him and had got lost for ever.

'Juliet!' The voice was nearer, at the door of the bothy, and it sounded very irritable and very human. Juliet raised her head and blinked at the dazzling beam of a powerful flashlight. Behind the flashlight loomed the head and shoulders of a man.

'Lance!' she exclaimed, and rising to her feet hobbled towards him. 'Oh, Lance, I thought I was lost for ever!'

She was in his arms and sobbing against the tweed of his jacket, crying because she was glad to see him, because he had come to find her. He held her silently, saying no words of comfort or endearment, but she could feel his hand on her head and then his fingers stroking her hair back from her face, touching the tears on her face.

At last her sobs subsided and he pushed her away from him, making her stand by herself. The beam of the flashlight flickered round the bothy as he inspected it and he asked curtly,

'Why didn't you answer when I called your name?'

'I thought it was the voice of the mist.'

'Voice of the mist? What the hell is that?' He sounded very cross and tired and her heart began to sink.

'Gareth told me that the mist has a voice which calls people to destruction and that you mustn't answer when it calls, or try to follow it, but stay put until the mist lifts and you can see your way.'

'Trust Gareth to have some nerve-racking tale like that to tell,' he grumbled.

'But it worked. I stayed put when I heard voices calling, and if I hadn't you wouldn't have found me.'

'I suppose that's one way of looking at it, but it would have been a damned sight quicker if you'd answered me. I've been calling you for the best part of an hour. I caught a glimpse of you when the mist lifted temporarily. Since then I've been following, or hoped I was following you. You have a hopeless sense of direction. You've been going round in circles. Let's sit down,' he added practically.

'But aren't we going back to the castle?' she asked as he pushed her into a chair and then pulled himself up on to the table. He stood the flashlight on the table so that its beam shone on the grimy whitewashed ceiling and reflected some light downwards. She could see him quite clearly, the bold nose, the contradictory mouth, the damp dark hair straggling over his forehead, and after several weeks of not seeing him she felt quite weak inside.

'Not yet. I'm tired and I notice that you're limping. Also the mist is still bad,' he replied. 'If we have to stay the night it won't be the first time we've stayed out together.'

He slanted a sardonic glance in her direction, but she managed to keep her face expressionless.

'Also, while we're alone and undisturbed,' he added, 'I'd be glad if you'd explain what's been going on at the castle to-day. I arrived to-night after the worst drive I've ever had through the hills to find everyone in a state of flap. Vinnie seemed to have lost her wits and kept rocking herself back and forth and muttering about her poor darling Maree being lost and how she should never have sent you out after her. Alison looked as if she'd shed enough tears to fill a reservoir. Gareth was locked in his room and wouldn't come out. In fact Mother was the calmest of all, but then she didn't know what had happened either. Then to make things worse, Maree walked in without you, so I came to look for you. Now tell me what's wrong with Gareth.'

'Didn't Alison tell you?' she asked warily.

'No. Maybe she was going to, but I didn't stop to listen when I realised you were out on the hills and probably lost.'

'She told him about Moira.'

'Why?' he rapped.

'She was angry because he's going away to Edinburgh and she thought I was going with him. You see,' this was going to be the most difficult part of all, telling him, 'she's in love with him,' she added in a low voice.

He was very still and very quiet sitting there on his hands staring at the floor of the bothy and not seeing it.

'And are you going with him to Edinburgh?' he asked, rather diffidently, she thought.

'No. He and I . . . I told you people can't love to order,' she said in a rush.

'So you did,' he replied heavily. 'I knew that he was going because he telephoned me. No one was more delighted than I was to hear that at last he'd come alive again. Does he know how Alison feels about him?'

'I don't know. I told her to go back and apologise to him for losing her temper and to tell him she loved him.'

'Maybe she tried and he wouldn't let her in.' He swore softly. 'Alison has always had trouble with her temper and it's often led her into saying what she shouldn't. If she hadn't lost it years ago it's possible Gareth wouldn't have married Moira.'

'Is it true what she said about Moira—about her being unfaithful and encouraging him to regard himself as a cripple for life?'

'Yes, it is.' Again there was a heaviness in his voice as if he was tired of the whole business, and longed to be away like an eagle soaring freely on the wind. 'And you have Alison to thank for unwittingly solving your mystery for you.'

'Not all of it. I still don't understand why you kept the truth from him and let him think badly of you instead.'

'You know I met Moira first and was sufficiently attracted to her to bring her home?' he asked.

'Yes. I suppose she was a stray cat.'

'What's that?' he demanded roughly.

'Alison said you were always bringing home stray cats. She said I was one.'

'It's a pity some women can't keep their mouths shut,' Lance grated. 'All right, I brought home a stray cat who turned out to be more of a tigress so that I wanted nothing more to do with her. But by then the damage was done and when my back was turned she went hunting Gareth. I was in Canada when the news came that she and Gareth were engaged. I wrote to him telling him he was a fool, but it had no effect. The invitation to the wedding came in the next post. Moira lost no time. I hadn't been working out there very long. I couldn't get leave, so I threw up my job and flew home, arriving on the day of the wedding. I tried to stop it.' He drew a sharp breath through gritted teeth. 'The foolish quixotic things one does in one's youth,' he

186

murmured, in self-disparagement. 'Everyone got the wrong idea, including my mother. They all thought I was in love with Moira and that I was jealous because she was marrying Gareth. I went to the wedding, and then caught the next plane back to Canada to hunt for another job. I couldn't bear to stay and see him being made a fool of.'

'But you came back later and helped to make a fool of him,' she accused.

'That was how it looked,' he agreed sombrely. 'That was how she arranged it to look. I was shocked by the bad effect his accident had on him, and I began to realise it was her fault and I was fool enough to take her out of his way once or twice in the hopes that he'd react. She didn't want him to recover. While he was disabled she could go off where she liked and with whom she liked—and believe me, she was never very particular with whom she went.'

'Did you take her to Chamonix?'

'No. She told Gareth she was going with me. She'd been telling him she'd been going with me for some time, but it didn't dawn on me what she'd been doing until I arrived at Chamonix and met her there. She was with a man. They were staying at another hotel. She came to see me and tried to persuade me not to tell Gareth about her latest little affair, but I refused. Next day she went up into the mountains and while she was up there she went skiing in spite of a warning. You know what happened after that—Graham told you. I took part in the rescue operation and made arrangements for her body to be flown home. I was going to tell Gareth everything, then I realised that he wasn't surprised I'd been there with her. She had told him she was going with me, and he trusted her with me. There was nothing I could say at a time like that when he was so grief-stricken, so I left it.'

'And let him go on believing she was perfect. That was why you didn't want me to find out what she'd done to him in case I told him.'

'Yes, and yet I've often wondered since whether I should have told him, whether it would have been kinder in the

187

end.' Lance shrugged his shoulders. 'Well, it's over now. Alison's spilled the beans and ten to one he'll blame me for not having told him before.'

'I'm glad she spilled the beans,' said Juliet.

'Glad, when you realise what Gareth must have gone through in the last few hours?'

'I wasn't thinking of him, I was thinking of you.'

'I'm afraid I don't understand.'

'Now you'll be able to put yourself first, you won't have to shield and protect Gareth any more from the truth about Moira,' she explained.

'I'm sorry, Juliet, but I'm not with you. Perhaps I'm more tired than I thought. The last weeks have been particularly hectic. I've been travelling a lot and I haven't caught up on my sleep. I was hoping that ... but I guess I was mistaken ...' He slid off the table and walked over to the door muttering, 'I'll see if the weather is improving.'

He had come hoping to have a few days' rest with Alison, and what had he found? thought Juliet. Alison in tears because she thought she had lost Gareth for the second time. Alison in love with Gareth and not with himself. What a blow to his hopes! No wonder he sounded dispirited.

But he hadn't stayed at the castle to comfort Alison. He had left her and, tired as he was, he had come through the mist to look for herself. She recalled the excited leap of her heart when she had recognised him standing in the doorway of the bothy. Was it possible she was in love too? In love with this enigmatic man who was so strangely quixotic in his own way?

'It's better outside,' he said, coming back to the table. 'Are you willing to risk it? Much as I'd like to spend the night here with you I'm concerned about Gareth.'

'There you go again,' Juliet blurted, suddenly angry with him. 'Putting him first instead of yourself. If you'd really like to spend the night here with me, why don't you?'

Her heart was beating madly. Never had she thought she would say such a thing to a man before!

She could tell by the glance that Lance flashed in her

direction that he was startled. But he wasn't at a loss for long. He half-sat on the table and leaned towards her.

'Sounds as if you're trying to seduce me, Juliet Grey,' he accused.

It was her turn to be startled. She hadn't realised how her suggestion might appear to him.

'I suppose it does,' she replied shakily.

'And do you think that's the way a sweet innocent girl like you should behave?'

'Oh, you're worse than Gareth at putting people on a pedestal. What makes you think I'm so innocent?'

'The look in your eyes, the shake in your voice.' He reached out a hand suddenly and touched her side under her left armpit. 'The frantic beating of your heart. You've never behaved like this before, and I'm wondering why I'm the target.'

'I thought you'd be able to guess, with those magical powers you have,' she countered.

'It's difficult to read a person's face in a dim light,' he mocked.

'There are other ways of finding out,' she whispered.

'Juliet, do you know what you're doing and saying?'

'Yes, I know. Thank you for coming to look for me. I've never been more glad to see anyone than I was to see you.'

It wasn't far to reach his cheek. Her kiss was feather-light, but it had the effect of dynamite.

'You mustn't do things like that,' he warned roughly.

'Why not?'

'Because it's bound to lead to something like this,' he retorted, and once again she felt the ruthlessness of his mouth on hers as he leaned forward and kissed her. A little later he asked, dryly,

'Are you going to slap my face?'

'No, because this time I think you mean it.'

'I meant it then. I told you I wanted to kiss you. I'd been wanting to kiss you ever since we tangled in the Cave of the White Rose. I did my best to keep my distance, thinking that it wouldn't do for me to fall in love with you if you loved my brother and if he loved you, but after dancing with you I couldn't help myself—and was socked on the jaw rather violently as a result.'

'Oh, I didn't mean to hurt you and I was sorry afterwards—but you see I thought you were doing it deliberately to stop me from going back and finding Graham,' exclaimed Juliet contritely. 'How foolish you must think me!'

'So foolish that I don't think I can let you wander about the world unprotected any more. You'll have to stay where I can keep an eye on you. You'll have to come and live with me.'

She eyed him doubtfully.

'Do you think that would be right?' she queried, and saw him grin.

'Yes, it will be right because I shall marry you first,' he replied. 'Which proves I must be in love with you, because I've never considered marrying anyone before. Have you ever been in love before?'

'How do you know I'm in love with you now?' she parried.

'I thought you might be the last time we talked together when you were quite obviously jealous of Alison but admitted you weren't in love with Gareth.'

'Oh, you!' she began furiously. 'Then why didn't you tell me you had fallen in love with me?'

'Because the time wasn't right. I wasn't sure, and you were all confused and hadn't long left off disliking me— and my cheek was still sore after being slapped.'

'Are you sure now?' she asked curiously.

'Yes, I wouldn't have set out to scour the misty moors in search of a white rose to take home with me, if I wasn't sure,' he murmured, taking her hand and pulling her to her feet. 'But let's stop beating about the bush. Will you marry me, Juliet?'

'Yes, I think so.'

'Only think so?'

'Yes, you see I'm not sure how to recognise when I'm in love.'

'It gets easier with practice,' he said with a ghost of a laugh, pulling her into his arms and trailing his lips across her cheek to her ear which he bit gently. 'And I promise to give you plenty of practice. But now we must go back to the castle and try and help Gareth and Alison. I have a feeling he might turn to her eventually, but first he has to recover his self-confidence fully and enjoy a little freedom of movement. Do you understand?'

'I understand,' Juliet answered soberly, and then suddenly she flung her arms around him and cried,

'Oh, Lance, I do love you, and I want to stay with you for ever.'

'Good. You're catching on fast,' he murmured, hugging her gently. Then taking her by the hand he led her out of the bothy into the soft starlit night in which there was no sign of mist, and down the hill to the castle.